Chairman Maria Boone sat back, stunned. There were six major galaxy clusters that consisted of about thirty-five galaxies that formed almost a clear pathway like rocks crossing a pond between the two. Of course there were a lot of other galaxies along the way, but that was the closest route jumping like the leading edge of Seeders expansion did.

The line of the big ghost ship went out and circled back to cross that path here in the Milky Way.

Could that have been the trail the Seeders used? If so, there were billions and billions and billions of Earth-like planets seeded with humans in those galaxies.

Was this big ship sent fourteen hundred thousand years ago as a message through time to the leading edge of the expansion?

And if so, why?

And why wasn't it stopping?

MORNING SONG

ALSO BY DEAN WESLEY SMITH

MORNING SONG

A SEEDERS UNIVERSE NOVEL

DEAN WESLEY SMITH

WMG
PUBLISHING

Morning Song
Copyright © 2022 by Dean Wesley Smith
Published in a different form in *Smith's Monthly #9*, June, 2014
Published by WMG Publishing
Cover and Layout copyright © 2022 by WMG Publishing
Cover design by Allyson Longueira / WMG Publishing
Cover art copyright © Philcold
ISBN-13: 978-1-56146-728-0
ISBN-10: 1-56146-728-6

For Kris
Because she likes this series for some strange reason

SECTION ONE:

IMPOSSIBLE MISSION

PROLOGUE

Wade ray stood calmly, waiting, his hands grasped behind his back as he stared at the huge view screen in front of him. His long gray hair flowed over his shoulders and covered the top of his casual gray silk shirt. He wore comfortable dark slacks and dark leather shoes. He never wore anything else.

He stood only six foot tall, had thin shoulders, and looked fairly young, but his mere presence in the ship's command center kept the other scientists behind him silent, staring at their individual control areas, some using screens, others using holographic heads-up displays.

The command center had three levels. The top level along the back had four stations, all diagnostic stations. The next level one step down had three major stations. Two were ship controls and operations, since the ship was huge, carrying over two thousand people.

The third and center chair was for the chairman of the ship, a term used by many to designate the captain of the ship. Most large Seeder ships like this one, with so many people and families, were for-profit businesses. So chairman was a better title for Wade Ray. Over the centuries, it had always been the standard designation on all Seeder ships.

Ray had stepped down to the area in front of his major control chair to try to get even slightly closer to the empty, black space staring at him on the screen.

Every human on this ship was a Seeder, working to spread the human race over every habitable planet in every galaxy they could reach.

The youngest scientist with him in the command center was only five hundred years old. Ray had told a few who asked that he had lived for just over three hundred thousand years, long enough to see humanity spread over six galaxies, including the Milky Way and its smaller satellite galaxies and now working into the Andromeda Galaxy and all its satellite galaxies.

But he was far older than even that.

He hoped to live long enough to see many more galaxies seeded as well, but he had no idea how long he would live. As far as he knew, barring accidents, Seeders could live forever, their bodies constantly renewing. Only boredom or accidents or violence cost Seeders their lives. That's why the mission of continuing to spread humanity from one galaxy to another was so important.

It kept them all sane. And challenged.

From what he understood, there were over fifty thousand major Seeder ships like his, mostly all working in the Andromeda Galaxy on the front lines of the Seeding. There were many, many other Seeders embedded in cultures without ship support working to help newborn human civilizations grow into stable cultures.

Seeders not only planted the human race, but spent centuries with each culture guiding each planet to maturity.

And not only could Seeders live a long time, but many had teleportation powers over short interstellar distances. It helped those without ships to get around between systems.

He had been embedded in cultures for many, many thousands of years, more than he could ever begin to remember, before taking command of his own ship. Now here, in this galaxy, his ship was one of the trouble-shooting ships who jumped around to where they were needed. He had no more desire to work the frontline of the Seeders. His interests lay with helping the cultures that the front line seeded grow.

Right now, he and his ship were back in the Larger Magellanic Cloud

Galaxy, a very long way from the Andromeda Galaxy and all its many satellite galaxies.

There was a problem here.

This Milky Way satellite galaxy had been seeded for a hundred thousand years now and had a stable and growing interstellar culture from which many had been recruited to become Seeders and help out in the Andromeda seeding.

The problem hadn't started here, but right now the problem was here and that's also why he was back across so much space.

Finally, a scientist to his left said, "Now."

As he had expected, a huge ship, thousands and thousands of times larger than his ship, almost unimaginable in size, dropped out of Trans-Tunnel flight, but didn't slow in the slightest as it flashed near the Parson's system near the outer edge of the Larger Magellanic Cloud Galaxy.

The ship was a perfectly proportioned winged ship, shaped like a glider, yet Ray could never imagine it entering any atmosphere since it was larger than most moons. It was normal older-Seeder-ship design, with a command bump near the front and the top of the pointed nose.

It was gray, without a mark or viewpoint or access port on it that anyone on his ship could find. It was as if the surface of the thing was one piece.

There didn't seem to be any engines or thruster ports or anything. Everything on the inside of that ship was hidden.

The huge ship was moving at an impossible real-space speed of over ninety-eight percent the speed of light.

If it followed its pattern as it had the numbers of times before, Ray knew it would remain in real space for two weeks real time, not ship time, and then jump back into trans-tunnel drive. It would appear again a hundred light years away, remain in real space for two real-time weeks again, then jump again.

Due to time and relativity problems, ship time on that ship was only about two days before it jumped. That was a problem with anything traveling that fast outside a trans-tunnel flight.

The ship had followed the exact same pattern since it was first discovered entering the Larger Magellanic Cloud Galaxy. He had watched it now for weeks.

Luckily, there had been no inhabited planets or systems in its way. It had plowed through a number of red dwarf systems, simply knocking anything aside that got it in its way with force screens of immense power.

Even a collision with a large moon had simply shattered the moon and hadn't even seemed to slow down or alter the big ship's course. That horrified him more than he wanted to let on and he felt responsible.

He knew it should be slowing. It wasn't.

Something was clearly wrong on that big ship and he had to figure out a way to stop it.

Beside him Tacita shook her head. She was feeling the same about this big ship as he was. They had to stop it.

Tacita had been at his side now for more years than he wanted to think about. They were partners in every sense of the word. It seems like they always had been.

She had long black hair that she always wore down and loose and dark black eyes that seemed to see everything.

She was also the smartest human on this ship by far. How she put up with him, he never understood and always questioned.

He could never imagine not having her with him, as his partner in life.

"Has it shifted course at all?" Ray asked, hoping something was changing as he stared at the huge ship on the screen in front of him.

The more his crew and others studied the ship, the more they all became convinced it was Seeder built, but long before any of their time with the Seeders.

He knew it was.

Many wondered if this ship might be from the original Seeders.

That possibility had many on this ship and other ships excited.

He and Tacita kept their silence. At this point they needed to.

"It has not shifted course," Tacita said, her voice clearly not happy with that. "Something is very wrong."

Ray could feel the knot in his stomach tighten even more.

The giant ship was on course for the Milky Way. And in a very short time it would plow through some of the most inhabited systems in the Milky Way Galaxy.

That was assuming it did not alter course, or if he couldn't find a way to alter its course or stop it.

Considering the shields that big ship had, the only way to alter that ship's course was to get inside of it. And at the speed it was going, with the shields it had, he had no idea how to do that.

None.

This was not supposed to be this way.

And none of his smartest scientists seemed to know what to do either.

Standing on the outside looking in was not something he liked or often did.

"Everyone have all the records you need?" he asked, turning to Tacita and the other scientists sitting at stations behind him.

Tacita nodded without looking up at him. He knew that she was scared to death of what the big ship would do when it reached the Milky Way Galaxy, the damage it would cause without ever meaning to.

"We have everything we need," Tacita said, again not looking up, but instead scanning the data on the screens in front of her station.

"Make sure we have two ships taking readings of that ship every time it appears and have them forward that data to us."

He hoped the big ship would start braking, but it should have before now if it was going to avoid disaster ahead.

"They are confirmed and will comply," Tacita said.

Ray nodded and stepped up and sat in his large chair, double-checking all the readings. Then with a glance at Tacita to his right, he said, "Get us to the Milky Way, on the predicted path ahead of this ship."

"Trans-tunnel jump in twenty seconds," Tacita said.

Staring at that big ship one more time, he said, "We got to go find some help. And maybe warn a few billion people to get out of the way."

This entire situation made him sick to his stomach.

"We have candidates that should be able to help," Tacita said.

He nodded.

Then as if he needed just one more look to really make his nightmares even more real, he kept staring at the huge glider-shaped ship until his ship jumped to trans-tunnel flight.

It would take them two days to cross the distance to the Milky Way. It would take the big ship six months.

Six very short months.

Before then they had better have some answers and some help, or billions of humans were going to die.

He was a Seeder. His job was to help start new human life and protect it and nurture it where he could.

There was just no way he was going to let a runaway ship destroy entire civilizations he had helped build.

CHAPTER 1

Chairman Maria Boone sat in her office, a dozen images of galaxies and possible paths through them marked in different colors floated in the air around her.

She had a cup of fresh green tea on her wood desk and the remains of a lunch consisting of fried chicken and fries shoved to one side, half eaten. The smell of chicken still filled the space, fighting with the smell of freshly brewing tea.

Beside the desk and comfortable desk chair that molded around her back and gave her perfect support, the other furniture in the room consisted of two chairs so people could sit facing her desk, a soft couch with a quilt tossed up over the back, and a coffee table in front of the couch.

The chairs and the coffee table were covered in data pads and the walls of the office were completely covered with two-dimensional maps of certain areas of space.

Today, she had her long red hair loose down her back and a pink tee-shirt on with the saying, "Don't Mess with the Redhead" on the front below a very large gun. She had a sports bra under the t-shirt and nylon shorts. At some point she planned on doing some exercise in the ship's big gym.

At least when she exercised, her freckles seemed to fade a little.

She was from a cold planet originally, where her light skin, golden eyes, and red hair had become almost the norm.

She hadn't been back there in a couple of centuries, but she kept thinking it might be fun, after all this time, to see how her world was progressing.

But at the moment, she was a couple galaxies away from her home world in the Lesser Magellanic Cloud. For over five years now, she and her crew and her ship had been backtracking the Seeders' route through what was called the Local Group of galaxies.

Over thirty galaxies were in the Local Group, including the three huge ones; the Milky Way Galaxy, the Andromeda Galaxy, and the Triangulum Spiral Galaxy. Over thirty satellite galaxies were gravitationally connected to one of the big three galaxies and the entire Local Group seemed to hold together as well.

Her goal was to find out if the Seeders had come into the Local Group or originated in it at some point in the distant past. That discovery would be worth a fortune to everyone on board. She was known as the top authority on Seeder history, which was why she had been able to organize this business and ship.

Everyone on board was a Seeder, but not one of them had started out that way. She sure hadn't. All six hundred souls on her ship had been recruited to the cause of spreading humanity through all of space at one point or another.

Of course, when someone joined on, they also got the gift of long life and health and a few other great gifts that came in handy at times. She was over four hundred years old now and still looked thirty, if that. Her long red hair still shined and the freckles that covered her face and shoulders never seemed to go away no matter what she did.

She kept wondering why Seeders could start millions of worlds with humans on them, solve the aging and sickness problem, and yet not find a solution for freckles.

All the information she and her crew had gathered in the last few months had seemed to conflict. Some data seemed to suggest that the Seeders had just come into the Local Sector, other data seemed to point to a single home planet where everything started out near the edge of the Local Group.

The problem was that the human planets in these smaller edge galaxies were all very mature and had little or no interest in Seeder history. She got help from them, but not much.

Now her ship was between galaxies, moving farther away from the Milky Way toward the edge of the Local Group. There was a small cluster of about a million stars there that might hold clues.

She was about to call it an afternoon in frustration when Dannie from Communications paged her.

She clicked off the images of the floating galaxies and said, "Yes."

"Chairman, I have a message from Chairman Wade Ray marked critical and for your eyes only."

"Thanks, Dannie," Maria said. "Put it through."

Maria brought the message up on her screen floating in the air in front of her before she even gave herself a moment to worry. She had no idea why Chairman Wade Ray would contact her. If the Seeders had an operating council, which they really did not, he would be the head of it. One of the most powerful of all the Seeders. And one of the oldest humans she knew about.

She couldn't imagine why he would even take notice of her.

The image came up and she could see the famous Chairman Ray smiling at her, but the smile didn't reach his eyes. His classic long, gray hair flowed down over his shirt and he looked thin and young, just as all Seeders did, even with the gray hair.

"Chairman Boone, I am sorry to have to pull you from your mission," he said. "But we have a situation developing in the Milky Way that needs your expertise."

She wished like hell this was an actual conversation so she could ask questions, but alas, it wasn't.

An image of a Seeder ship came up on the screen. It looked old, as some of the early Seeder ships she had studied. And there was something else wrong about the image.

Ray's voice came over the image. "Please note the small dot against the lower right portion of the right wing of this ship."

She leaned forward, staring at what looked like a dot against the hull of the old ship.

Then the image started to zoom in and it took her mind a moment to realize just what she was seeing. That just wasn't possible.

"That dot is my ship, one of the largest ships we have at this time, in comparison to the large ship behind it," Ray said, confirming what she knew couldn't be possible. Space allowed for the building of huge ships, but that huge ship could hold an entire planet's population and have room left over, it was so big.

"The big ship seems to be out of control and it has extremely powerful screens," Ray said. "It will plow through many inhabited planets in the Milky Way, killing billions, if it can't be stopped."

Ray's face appeared again. "I have sent all the data we have gathered about this ship and its path. We are going to try to board the ship to gain control of it, since we fear it is a ghost ship. We need your expertise on this coming mission."

Then Chairman Wade Ray nodded. "Please help us. Billions of lives are at stake."

At that the message ended.

She sat and listened to it one more time, then did a quick glance at all the data. Maybe, just maybe, she didn't have to backtrack any more to find the path of the original Seeders. Maybe the knowledge had come to them.

She had Dannie send back a short message to Chairman Ray. "Message received. We are on the way."

Then she paged her five senior staff and told them to meet her in the Command Center. At top trans-tunnel speed it would take them almost two weeks to reach The Milky Way and the location where Chairman Ray had asked for them to go.

In that two weeks they had a lot of planning to go.

And research, since that ship's path might point back to the solution they have been looking for on this entire mission as to where the Seeders started from.

But first she wanted to have her senior staff all see the message from Chairman Ray at the same time. She wanted to see their reactions.

And then eventually everyone on board would see the message and data as well. After all, they were all in this together.

But with so many lives at stake, she couldn't imagine a single member of her crew having an issue with returning to the Milky Way and trying to help.

They were all Seeders, after all. Starting, protecting, and nurturing human life was their job.

CHAPTER 2

Roscoe Mundy brushed the long brown hair from off his face and looked around, stunned at what he saw. He was alone and he stood in the center of the huge main room of an old lodge. He had been in some pretty impressive structures over the last few hundred years, especially the last twenty years working implanted as an enforcer with Sector Justice in the third sector of the Milky Way Galaxy, but this building was close to the top in impressiveness of pure comfort of all the places he had seen.

He dropped his small leather pack on the wooden plank floor and took a deep breath of the clean air. He had on a long-sleeved black shirt with a black leather vest over the top of it and the sleeves rolled up. He had on cowboy boots and jeans and a wide, black-leather belt. The belt buckle was two pistols crossed like swords.

He stood in one place in the big room, just looking around, trying to take in the details.

The walls, posts, and beams were peeled and polished logs that had to be ten feet around in places. A giant, smooth-rock fireplace filled one side of the immense room, a natural crackling fire going in it, giving the room a wonderful, wood-smoke smell.

What looked like a check-in desk, all made out of polished wood, filled the right side of the room near a grand, wood staircase that wound up to a floor above.

To the right of where he had transported in were brown cloth couches and chairs, all facing the huge fireplace and looking very comfortable and deep, with quilts tossed over the backs of a few of them.

He could see pine trees outside the huge windows in a neighboring dining room area that had a good twenty tables with four chairs each. None of the tables were set.

This lodge was very high up in some coastal mountains on a planet that had had a major accident. A stray electromagnetic pulse from a distant nova had wiped out all but about a million of its population. That disaster had happened just over three hundred years before, just after he joined the Seeders and came to the Milky Way to help out.

The population of the planet was recovering nicely, especially in such a short time. In fact, they were almost back into space. They did not know anything about the huge galaxy-wide society of humans growing beyond their system, but eventually they would and join in.

Clearly, this lodge was from the period before the accident, and had been amazingly preserved by someone.

But this planet seemed to be jinxed in more ways than just a freak electromagnetic pulse storm. Now this planet was in a direct line of a speeding monster ghost ship that would destroy it as if nothing were there.

He had been recruited by Chairman Wade Ray to help stop the ghost ship. That's why he was here.

He picked up his leather overnight bag and moved over to one of the big, overstuffed chairs near the left side of the fireplace. He dropped into the chair, enjoying how it felt completely comfortable and natural.

He leaned back and just stared up at the ceiling and the large, wooden logs over his head.

"Amazing, isn't it?" a man said as he came down the staircase.

"Completely," Roscoe said, looking over at the man.

Roscoe had a sudden moment of surprise looking at the smiling, thin guy who looked like a scientist in a brown, pullover sweater and cloth pants and loafers. They guy even wore glasses, even though no Seeder he had ever met needed them.

All Seeder health was perfect. A benefit of the job.

Roscoe couldn't remember the guy's name, but they had met once before about a hundred years ago, trying to stop a war in the first sector. Roscoe hadn't realized the guy was a Seeder at the time.

"Nice seeing you again, Mr. Mundy," the guy said, extending his hand as he got close. "My name is Vardis Fisher. Everyone just calls me Fisher."

Roscoe stood and shook his head. "Just call me Roscoe. Didn't know you were a part of all this when we were back in Sector One."

"I didn't know you were either," Fisher said, smiling and dropping into a chair across from Roscoe. "Maybe they should put bells on us or something."

"Name tags," Roscoe said, smiling. "Never was good with names and after a couple of centuries, that's gotten worse."

Fisher laughed and indicated the big lodge around them. "Like the old place?"

"I sure do," Roscoe said. "All yours?"

"My wife and I sort of met here about three hundred years ago," Fisher said. "This lodge saved her and we were recruited by the Seeders at that point to help out. We've kept the lodge as our home and base ever since."

"Nice," Roscoe said. He had thought of finding a home base at some point, but so far it just hadn't come up since he moved around so much. The longest he had stayed in any one place was with Sector Justice, and he knew that was almost over as well, since he couldn't explain not aging.

But a big lodge like this one with extreme privacy was certainly something he could enjoy. Someday he would find a permanent home.

At that moment, Chairman Wade Ray, his wife Tacita, and two other women materialized in the open area in the center of the room.

Every time Roscoe saw Wade Ray, he was impressed and stunned. Ray was extremely old and powerful among the Seeders. Roscoe had no idea how old he really was and had never had the chance to actually ask. He didn't look old except for the long, gray hair that hung down over his expensive silk shirt.

Both of the other women were stunningly good looking. One had dark, short hair and the other long red hair. The dark-haired one went over and kissed Fisher, so that had to be his wife, Callie.

The redhead just stood there wearing a t-shirt that left little to the imagination and tight jeans and running shoes. Clearly the woman was in amazing shape and her face and neck and arms were covered in freckles that made her look cute and very alluring.

And she had large golden eyes that were amazing. So far they hadn't looked at him, as she was too busy looking around at the lodge. He felt lucky because if she did look at him, he wasn't sure he would be able to turn away.

He hadn't felt that attracted to someone else in a long, long time. He would have to be very careful around her because all he really wanted to do was play connect the dots with his tongue on those freckles.

He forced himself to take a deep breath, clear that thought, and turn his attention to Chairman Ray and his black-haired wife Tacita. She had done a quick look of the lodge and nodded, then moved over to the couch and sat down, saying nothing.

Roscoe knew her reputation as being cold and brilliant. It was rumored that she and Chairman Ray had been a team for over a hundred thousand years. He couldn't imagine being with one woman for that long. He couldn't imagine living that long, actually. In fact, that number just sort of numbed him, it was so large.

As they all got seated, Roscoe kept his attention on Chairman Ray, but noticed out of the corner of his eye that the redheaded woman had now noticed him and was staring at him. He didn't dare let himself look at her.

He wanted to, but he didn't dare.

"This is our command team," Chairman Ray said. "Welcome. You've all been briefed on what we face, so first let me do some introductions and reasons why I have asked you to be part of this."

He turned to Fisher. "Chairman Vardis Fisher and his partner and wife, Callie Sheridan. Both of them are more educated than most anyone you will ever meet. They will run the science part of this mission, from mathematics to the social sciences. We have no idea what we might find when we get inside that ship, so we need to be ready for anything and

they have two of the most diverse and nimble minds I have had the pleasure to meet."

Both Fisher and Callie nodded to that, clearly slightly embarrassed.

Chairman Ray went on. "Their ship and two other scientific ships
will be support and they will lead the scientists."

Then Chairman Ray turned to the redhead. "This is Chairman Maria
Boone."

Roscoe looked at her, but she had her golden eyes focused on
Chairman Ray.

"Chairman Boone is the leading authority on the history of the original Seeders," Ray said, "and she and her ship cut a tracking research trip
short and returned from the edge of the Local Group boundary to help.
Since that old ship is an ancient Seeders' ship, we're going to need her
entire crew of experts to unravel what we find."

Then Chairman Ray turned to Roscoe. "This is Roscoe Mundy who
doesn't know it yet, but has become Chairman Mundy of a ship called
The Huntington. It has just reached orbit above us."

Roscoe managed to not jerk from surprise, but instead nodded a
thank-you to Chairman Ray.

Roscoe had had no intention of becoming a Chairman of his own ship
this soon. In a few hundred years of more experience, maybe, but not
yet. But it seemed he was being given a gift for the moment. He just
hoped he was up for the task.

"*The Huntington* is the heaviest-armed Seeder ship ever built. It was
recently finished and stored in the First Sector, waiting for a moment
when it would be needed. So Chairman Mundy will be in charge of all
military and security forces we might need going into that large ship. He
is one of the clearest-thinking military brains we have."

Roscoe nodded to that. He had been briefed on that part of the
mission, just not being a Chairman of his own ship. Nor had he expected
the compliments coming from Chairman Ray.

"Four other Seeder military ships will be joining us from the
Andromeda Galaxy," Ray said, "as soon as they can get here, which will
be in about two weeks."

Roscoe nodded, suddenly totally overwhelmed. He had no doubt he
was going to have to recruit a few mortals from Sector Justice into the

Seeders, with permission, of course, to help on his ship. He had no idea how to do any of that.

Seeders Justice was a fairly new policing organization that had formed in the Milky Way Galaxy. It had a lot of great people in it, experienced people he could trust.

Chairman Ray then patted the leg of his wife. "Tacita and I will be in overall command of this mission. You all will report to me or Tacita."

All four of them nodded.

Nodding right now was about all Roscoe could do. Mostly he kept his focus on the patterned carpet in front of his chair.

"We're going to have to work together if we're going to save billions of lives," Ray said. "The big ship will hit the edge of the Milky Way Galaxy in five months. It will destroy this planet in six months and ten days if we can't stop it or alter its course."

"We have a very real ticking clock," Fisher said.

"Very real," Chairman Ray said, his voice soft.

No one said a word as the fire in the big stone fireplace crackled.

CHAPTER 3

Maria Boone had almost melted in her chair when she stopped looking at the incredible lodge they were in and noticed Roscoe Mundy. She had never had a reaction to a man like that before and luckily she had had a few minutes to recover as Chairman Ray introduced them all and outlined their mission.

And watching Mundy get surprised with his own command of a ship was amazing. He actually managed to stay calm, but she could tell from how he shifted twice when Ray wasn't watching, he was trying his best to gather himself.

He was cool and very smooth and stunningly handsome. Wow. Who knew she would be attracted to the military type. His long brown hair sure didn't make him look military.

Finally, it was Chairman Fisher who broke the silence after Ray's announcement of how little time they had.

"Any ideas how we are going to get inside that thing?" Fisher asked.

Maria pulled her gaze from Roscoe, who was still managing to look at the floor in front of him as he gathered himself.

"We have a few ideas," she said, "from plans of other older Seeder ships that have come down through the centuries. But we'll have to work with you to confirm our theories. And from what we can tell from the readings of the shield, teleporting inside isn't an option."

"We have come to the same conclusion," Ray said.

"I am one hundred percent convinced," Callie said, "that this is an old Seeder ship. But in all the records we have ever seen, there has been no real mention of building something this large. So this might be very old, or very new."

Ray nodded to her that she should go on. And Tacita looked up and focused her intense gaze on Maria.

"New?" Roscoe asked, now clearly recovered.

She looked at him and somehow managed to not just stare into those deep, dark eyes. He held her gaze, but he seemed as surprised as she was with the tension between them.

And the attraction.

"It's a possibility," she said, nodding, then pulling her gaze from Roscoe back to Ray and Tacita. "I'm not convinced that early Seeders had this kind of capability. I don't think we do now unless there is something I don't know."

Ray just nodded.

Maria went on. "If the Seeders originated outside the Local Group of galaxies as many think, then their civilization now would be very old and capable of this kind of technology. And might still be using this older design."

Again, Ray and Tacita just nodded.

"It seems there is a second problem in boarding the big ship," Roscoe said. "It's traveling faster than anything I know of when it drops out of trans-tunnel drive."

"With some modifications by my chief engineer, my personal jump ship can match that speed exactly," Fisher said. "My jump ship is small, and can only hold about twenty comfortably, but it can match the speed without a problem."

Maria watched as Roscoe nodded.

"I would like to attempt the first boarding in three weeks," Chairman Ray said.

He then turned to Fisher and Callie. "Thank you for the kind offer of the use of your wonderful lodge as we prepare."

"Feel free to come and go," Callie said.

"We have stocked the kitchen at the bottom of the stairs," Fisher said. "Help yourself."

Maria loved the idea of spending the next weeks coming and going from this lodge. That sounded heavenly after the year she had just spent onboard her ship.

Chairman Ray and Tacita stood, forcing all of them to their feet out of respect.

"We meet back here tomorrow for breakfast at 8 a.m. planet time," Ray said. "That is sixteen hours from now exactly."

Maria nodded, as did everyone else.

"Keep your ships shielded and cloaked," he said. "The locals on this planet will detect it otherwise."

Then Ray turned to Roscoe. "Chairman Mundy, come with me and I'll give you a tour of your new command."

With a quick nod, Roscoe smiled at her and then the three of them vanished.

That smile almost took her breath away. Wow, he was something.

Maria turned to Fisher and Callie. "Thank you for your hospitality. I'll see you tomorrow morning."

"You are more than welcome," Callie said. "This is our home we're trying to save so glad this is being taken so seriously."

Maria nodded. "We'll save it."

With that she transported back to her ship, hoping that they actually could.

And hoping beyond hope that she could find time with Chairman Mundy. Private time.

CHAPTER 4

Roscoe finished the quick tour of his ship in the Command Center of *The Huntington*. The big Command Center felt at home to him instantly and scared him to death at the same time.

The ship was huge and had firepower that could take down an entire planet if it needed to. Roscoe hoped it would never come to that.

Ever.

But from what he had seen of the big ship coming into the galaxy, nothing *The Huntington* had in firepower would even dent it.

The ship already had a full engineering crew and some basic officers who had gotten it here, but they were not as trained as he would like.

"I have dinner to eat, and you have some core crew in the mess," Ray said, smiling, after he gave him the quick rundown of the Command Center. "They all will head certain areas of your ship and one is your second-in-command. Might want to go meet them to help you get started."

Then smiling, Ray vanished, leaving Roscoe stunned at not only being in charge of such an amazing warship, but that he already had some command crew. He knew the ship needed a basic crew of a hundred to just limp along, which it had now, mostly in engineering and communications, but three hundred would be better.

He had a couple of weeks to get that many in place and no idea how to do that. Now it sounded like he had some help.

He took a deep breath and looked around at the three-level Command Center. His station was in the center of the second level. One entire wall was a giant screen in front of his station. It didn't feel right to go sit in the chair just yet. Maybe tomorrow.

So instead, he took a deep breath and transported to the mess.

Four people were sitting there on the far side of the huge room, around a table near the kitchen door. They were all eating and laughing. Two were men, two women.

The place smelled wonderfully of hamburgers and fries. And they all seemed to have milkshakes in front of them. Clearly the ship had some kitchen crew already. One more detail to not worry about.

Roscoe's stomach rumbled, making him realize he needed to try to eat as well.

He started through the sea of empty tables toward the group of four when he suddenly realized he knew one of them. He would know that shaved head and long nose anywhere.

Jonas Craig, his second-in-command at Sector Justice, the police force that watched over different parts of the Milky Way, sector by sector. Sector Justice knew nothing about Seeders being in their midst. They still believed that all Seeders had done their work and just moved on. Which was mostly true, but not completely.

Jonas was one of the best fighters Sector Justice had and could kill a man with a single finger. They had worked together now for ten years and Roscoe had trusted him with his life. How was that possible that Jonas was a Seeder as well?

"Jonas, you're kidding me, right?" Roscoe said as he moved toward them.

Jonas turned from the others, staring and clearly stunned, his mouth open showing a half-chewed hamburger. Then Jonas blinked twice and closed his mouth.

So Jonas hadn't known Roscoe was a Seeder either. Amazing.

The other three turned and Roscoe recognized them all, even though he didn't know their names. All were from different branches of the Sector Justice force.

It seemed the Seeders were in just about everything when it came to keeping the peace and making sure human populations they had planted progressed in a peaceful way.

Jonas finally gathered himself enough to finish chewing, stand and face Roscoe. "Damn, I'm glad to see you," he said, smiling.

"Not half as much as I am to see you," Roscoe said, smiling. "I didn't know you were a Seeder."

Jonas laughed. "I didn't know the same about you. Go figure."

They both laughed.

The others stood to greet him and with that, Jonas turned to introduce him to the other three. And he started with "Folks, this is Chairman Mundy."

And that once again just shocked Roscoe more than he wanted to admit.

CHAPTER 5

By the time she finished a quick dinner in her office, alone, Maria managed to somehow get her mind away from Roscoe Mundy and back on the task at hand.

The guy was amazing and she couldn't believe a military type had caught her attention like that.

Yet she so wanted to just get to know him, and maybe a few other things with that incredible body of his as well. It had been far too long since she had a man in her life. She didn't want to think about exactly how long.

Using three-dimensional images projected into the air in her office, she had the big ship's course in a dotted line as it headed for the Milky Way.

In the research on the ship on the way back to the Milky Way, what she noticed about that dotted line was that on short distances, it seemed straight, but over much, much larger distances, it had a very, very slight continuous curve that could be projected backwards.

Every day the course shifted in a slight amount that over hundreds and hundreds of years mounted up to about one percent.

So shrinking down the known area of space to galaxies being nothing more than points in the air in her office, she extended the past course of the big ship.

It would take, at the ship's speed, about three million years for the ship to make a complete circle return to where it started.

Her only problem was that she wasn't sure how long the ship had been going. Any point on the circle could have been its launch point.

So starting with a hundred years ago, she had her computer show her the path of the ship through space.

It didn't come close to any galaxy or even small star cluster at that point, allowing for the speed and direction of the galaxies movements.

She repeated the same over and over and over, taking her time to make sure she didn't miss any detail.

It seemed to always go between star clusters and galaxies as if the course had been carefully planned to have nothing run into the big ship.

It became clear as she went that the big ship's encounter with the two galaxies so far in the Local Group was almost a fluke.

Or planned, one or the other.

She was starting to bet on planned.

In sixty thousand years, the big ship hadn't come close to any group of stars or galaxies at all.

Nothing.

It had traveled in the big expanse between galaxies, missing everything as it went.

That just seemed wrong and almost impossible, so maybe at some point the big ship had changed course. She couldn't imagine the scale she was looking at, yet she knew that the Seeders had been in the Local Group galaxies for about five hundred thousand years that it took to do the twelve small galaxies and the Milky Way.

It had taken the Seeders an amazingly short period of only fifty thousand years to do most of the seeding in the Milky Way. But at around fifty thousand years per large galaxy, and over thirty galaxies in the Local Group, it was going to take over a million years to work through them all and head on outside the Local Group.

No way her brain could grasp living that long, but she assumed it was possible. She just couldn't imagine it.

She had heard that some of the Seeders working the frontlines of the Seeding were older than Chairman Ray if that was possible.

Seeding entire galaxies was such an immense project, she just couldn't grasp it all, even though she was a Seeder and understood every step in the process. Her perspective was still on hundreds of years, which felt stunningly long. A thousand years seemed impossible, and three hundred thousand just wasn't possible to understand, just like the distances of space she was staring at.

So she kept going, trying to change her perspective on time. She tried to make herself believe she understood the scale of space just fine. Time, on the other hand, was difficult for her to grasp.

At eight hundred thousand years back, the big ship was finally in a position to brush past the side of a small satellite galaxy of a larger cloud of galaxies.

But it was only a brush and the ship would have had no reason to leave that galaxy in the direction it had started. So she was pretty sure that wasn't its starting point.

At one million, four hundred thousand years, she finally found what she thought might make sense. The ship went through the edge of a smaller satellite galaxy coming from solidly inside an even larger spiral galaxy.

The ship had completed just under one half of its circle managing to miss everything along the way.

She had the Local Group including the Milky Way galaxy floating on one side of her office in very tiny scale, then she put up this large spiral galaxy in another corner in small scale as well.

Then she had her computer put up all the galaxy formations between the two. Then she asked the computer to show the closest path from the one spiral galaxy to the Local Group and the Milky Way.

She sat back, stunned. There were six major galaxy clusters that consisted of about thirty-five galaxies that formed almost a clear pathway like rocks crossing a pond between the two. Of course there were a lot of other galaxies along the way, but that was the closest route jumping like the leading edge of Seeders expansion did.

The line of the big ship went out and circled back to cross that path here in the Milky Way.

Could that have been the trail the Seeders used? If so, there were billions and billions and billions of Earth-like planets seeded with humans in those galaxies.

Was this big ship sent fourteen hundred thousand years ago as a message through time to the leading edge of the expansion?

And if so, why?

And why wasn't it stopping?

Clearly, if it was meant to come here, something had gone wrong in its braking plans after all those years.

But nothing about any of this made any sense at all.

She recorded everything and then glanced at the time. She only had seven hours before she needed to be on the planet below for a meeting.

She needed to show all of them the data. It might not be right, but if it was, they needed to approach this ship very, very differently than they would approach a ghost ship.

But one thing she was sure of. This Seeder ship was at least one-point-four million years old.

At least.

But from a very, very advanced Seeder culture.

CHAPTER 6

Roscoe couldn't believe how good a cook Fisher was, and how stunningly beautiful Maria looked in the morning.

He was sitting across from her and eating breakfast in the wonderful café that seemed to fill the basement of the old lodge.

The café had been perfectly preserved over the years and had two u-shaped counters that stuck out into the room with thirty or so bar stools with cloth seats along the counters. The person waiting on them, in this case, Fisher, walked down the center of the counters.

The room had low log ceilings and huge windows that looked out into a vast forest of very old pine trees. The sun was sending rays of light down into the dense underbrush and forest floor that slanted away from the lodge.

Since the end of the counter was curved, all six of them could see each other fine. Ray and Tacita sat on the two chairs at the end of the counter. Roscoe and Fisher on one side, when Fisher stopped serving and sat down.

Maria sat across from Roscoe near Callie, clearly enjoying her eggs and ham as much as he was. She had smiled at him when they arrived and said hello, but nothing else.

Luckily she hadn't said much else. He would have had a hard time talking, since she affected him so much. He really needed to get past that problem if they all were going to work together.

There was an amazing attraction between them, and if they weren't trying to save a few billion lives, he might be trying to get close to her right now. If they did save these planets, there would be time. They were both Seeders, they had lots of time.

But that didn't mean he didn't want to get to know her better. Much, much better.

He had spent most of the time since their last meeting with his start-up crew, working to figure out his new ship and build plans on recruiting.

Since they were all from the Sector Force that consisted mostly of trained fighters that guarded the Milky Way sector by sector, they all felt comfortable recruiting top staff from that. But they would not take so many as to leave Sector Justice depleted.

Some of the most advanced cultures in the first sector, meaning the first sector of the Milky Way seeded, had some top militaries as well. That would be good recruiting grounds as well.

They might not have *The Huntington* fully staffed in three weeks, but they would be able to fly and fight if they had to.

So after only six hours of uneasy sleep in his new command cabin, which was huge and had no personal touches at all yet, he had managed to be on time to the meeting with Chairman Ray and the others.

Roscoe was almost done eating the fantastic eggs, soft toast, and melt-in-his mouth ham when Maria pushed her plate away and turned slightly to face Chairman Ray, who we also just finishing.

"I have something I think we all need to talk about."

Roscoe loved the sound of her voice. It was firm and solid and slightly deeper than he would have expected coming from someone only about five-four and with so many freckles.

"Start us off, Chairman Boone," Ray said, nodding.

Maria set up a small device on the counter in front of her and Fisher, who was standing inside the u-shape of the counter eating, quickly moved to take her plate and dirty silverware.

She touched the top of the device. In the air over the counter between them and the kitchen, an image of the Local Group of galaxies appeared.

Roscoe recognized it at once and even knew where in the spiral arms of the Milky Way they were now located and the area of his home world in a small satellite galaxy near to, and almost touching, the Milky Way.

At times he had trouble grasping the size and scale of the entire Milky Way, but he was slowly, over the last centuries, coming to realize how impressive the Seeders were. And how lucky he had been to be recruited into their ranks.

"There are theories that are pretty solid that the leading edge of the Seeders entered the Local Group of galaxies here," Maria said.

She had one of the small cloud galaxies in the group near one side brighten.

Roscoe nodded to himself. That was the theory he had heard as well.

"That was about five hundred thousand years ago," Maria said.

Roscoe noticed that both Ray and Tacita nodded, but said nothing.

Maria went on. "If we follow the pattern of Seeders, we tend to jump as we move forward to the closest next galaxy or star cluster and then move on, like we are doing now into Andromeda and its satellite galaxies, leaving behind many of us to help and protect and guide the forming seeded civilizations."

Everyone again nodded. All basic stuff that Roscoe understood. Clearly Maria was trying to put down a foundation of what she was going to say.

"It takes around fifty thousand years to just do the initial seeding of each normal galaxy, give or take depending on size and numbers of suitable planets."

Roscoe knew that as well, but always had a hard time imagining covering an entire galaxy such as the Milky Way in only fifty thousand years.

"So I extended out the pattern outside the Local Cluster," Maria said, "going from closest to closest galaxy and this is what I got over a one-point-eight million year period of time, assuming the pace of Seeding remained about the same as it has through the Local Group."

The scale of the image of Local Group floating in the air in the diner came down slightly as other galaxies and galaxy groups were added like steps ending in a large spiral galaxy that looked a lot like the Milky Way and Andromeda.

Roscoe had no idea how far that was away and he didn't want to ask. Even if someone said the number, he wouldn't be able to grasp what it meant. He just knew it was a very, very long distance, but yet that galaxy was in the relative neighborhood of the Milky Way in comparison to the entire universe.

Still, the number of years she was talking about just stunned him. Did he really belong to an organization that started almost two million years before?

Chairman Ray was nodding, so Maria went on.

"This is the track of the big ship."

She put a dotted yellow line showing the track of the big ship entering the local cluster.

"The ship is actually turning slightly, but at such a small amount that it takes just at one thousand years to make a one degree shift in course."

"It's turning?" Fisher asked, clearly as surprised as Roscoe felt.

"Not enough to be noticeable over a year, but over one hundred years, yes."

Roscoe looked over at Chairman Ray and Tacita, but both just sat listening.

"So if we extend out the line the ship is traveling on," Maria said, "we get this. Again, note, in one-point-four million years, the big ship comes near no other galaxy or star cluster until it hit the Local Group here. That had to be planned."

Again the scale of all the galaxies came down as the dotted yellow line went out near the edge of the room, slowly turning until it ran smack into the middle of the big spiral galaxy that in theory the Seeders had come from.

"That's one-point-four million years of travel for the ship," Maria said. "One-point-eight million years ago, the Seeders started on this seeding path, which would be sure to lead to the Local Group and the Milky Way if they continued onward."

Everyone was silent. Roscoe just stared at what she was showing them.

Then Ray spoke softly. "So about one-point-four million years ago, from that galaxy, they launched this big ship to intercept the leading edge of their seeding."

36

Roscoe didn't know what to think. He was having a difficult time grasping time and the scale of distance.

But he did have one question he needed to ask. "With the time dele- tion that ship is experiencing, we know from an outside take, it took one- point-four million years if it was launched from there."

He pointed to the spiral galaxy that intersected the path of the big ship.

Maria nodded and Roscoe could see both Fisher and Callie's eyes get big as they caught his question ahead.

"If someone, or a group of people are inside that ship," Roscoe asked, "how old would they be?"

Ray just stared at him, as did those wonderful golden eyes of Maria.

Finally Fisher answered his question. "About two hundred thousand years old, give or take."

"Younger than we are," Tacita said bluntly.

Roscoe just couldn't imagine that, so he pushed the idea of even trying to imagine it out of his mind.

"But why would anyone undertake such a journey?" Callie asked, "assuming there is anyone alive in there and it's not just a robot ship."

That question just hung there in the air along with all the small images of vast galaxies and a dotted line of an impossible journey.

"My question exactly," Maria said. "At our full trans-tunnel speed, going directly from that galaxy to this one would take about nine hundred years is all. So doing this makes no sense."

Roscoe had nothing more to ask or even say. His mind was over- whelmed.

Across from him, Maria sat down and clicked off her device and the galaxies floating in the air vanished.

Ray looked around at everyone, then nodded to Maria. "Great job, Chairman Boone."

Maria nodded, but didn't smile. Roscoe had a hunch his question just tossed in another dimension to the reality of her specialty of tracing back the Seeder's path.

Ray looked at his wife and then at Fisher. "Thank you for the wonderful breakfast. May we impose on you again tomorrow at the same time?"

"Of course," Fisher said nodding.

"He loves cooking almost more than anything else," Callie said.

"Good," Ray said. "I think we need to adjourn until then to think about what Chairman Boone has presented and continue preparing for our first boarding attempt."

Then with a nod to Fisher again, Chairman Ray and Tacita vanished.

"That was amazing," Roscoe said to Maria.

"And that was a great question I hadn't thought about," Maria said.

They stared at each other for a moment and Roscoe couldn't think of a thing to say. The attraction to Maria was more than he could remember ever feeling before.

Fisher and Callie both started to clean up, so finally breaking his gaze from those fantastic golden eyes, Roscoe stood and took his plate and empty orange juice glass and headed for the kitchen.

"I'll be glad to wash," he said.

"And I'll dry," Maria said from behind him.

"And we'll take you both up on that," Callie said, laughing.

Suddenly Roscoe wasn't sure what he had gotten himself into. But he liked the idea of spending a little more time with Maria.

If he could manage to not break any dishes.

CHAPTER 7

Maria really enjoyed the short time she had standing beside Roscoe at the sink in the old lodge. Every so often their hands would touch as he handed her a plate, and each time it felt like a small shock.

He kept glancing at her the entire time as well.

He was so damned good-looking, and it had been so long since she had even allowed herself to look at another man. She didn't dare look at her crew as the Chairman of the ship, and she hadn't spent much time away from her ship in some time.

So maybe she was just desperate. But she didn't think so. Roscoe was handsome and funny and clearly very, very smart.

Callie had excused herself and transported to their ship and Fisher had stayed in the kitchen to clean up the grill, and bring them the remains of the dishes from the counter.

Roscoe had quizzed Fisher on the lodge and then got both of them laughing with his incredible sense of humor.

In a moment when Fisher had gone back into the diner area to make sure they hadn't missed a dish, Roscoe turned to her. "So how far out were you when Chairman Ray recalled you to help with this?"

She laughed. "Far out describes it," she said. "We had gone through three seeded galaxies and were on the other side of the third headed toward a small group of stars at the edge of the Local Group."

"Wow," he said, shaking his head, causing his long brown hair to swirl back and forth on his collar which took her a moment to pull her attention away from and back to the plate in her hand.

"I can't even imagine that," he said, focusing on scrubbing out a pot in the sink like an expert, "yet from what you were talking about, it's a small distance compared to what that huge ship has crossed."

"A very small part," she said. "And it still took us two full weeks at full drive to get back."

"Were the human populations of those galaxies you went through extremely advanced?" Roscoe asked her.

"They were, and very peaceful," she said, remembering some of the encounters. "But we really didn't introduce ourselves as Seeders and none of them had speeds of ships high enough to cross the distances between galaxies. And we didn't tell them we could."

"Wow, sort of trapped in their own galaxy," Roscoe said. "How strange that sounds."

Maria had to admit, it did sound strange. "What was weird was that none of them much cared about the Seeders. They had just come to accept thousands and thousands of years before that Seeders had all moved on and that Seeders couldn't be followed. In fact, the farther out we went, the more Seeders were just myths relegated to deep archives of past religions."

"I don't feel like a religion, do you?" Roscoe asked.

"Honestly wouldn't know what a religion would feel like," she said, laughing.

"I don't either," he said, taking a towel to dry off his hands as he looked at her with a sly smile. "But I'm betting sort of soft and squishy."

She laughed and said, "And slick and hard to hold onto."

He managed to keep a straight face on that handsome face for a moment before breaking into laughter that, if she had her way, she would listen to a lot more of over time.

CHAPTER 8

Roscoe spent the next two weeks mostly with Jonas, working with staffing and training the crew for *The Huntington*.

They had decided to mostly stay with Seeders and not recruit too many new humans right out of the blue. In fact, of the two hundred they picked, only ten were non-Seeders. Five couples.

One such couple was the most famous couple in all of Sector Justice, Mattie Silks and Red Kenney. Red owned another organization that worked closely with Sector Justice called Innocence Inc. Mattie was rumored to be the most deadly enforcer in all of Sector Justice and had taken the job as liaison between the two organizations when she and Red were married.

He and Jonas both knew them and had approached them on their private ship. It didn't take long to convince them after showing them the big ship and telling them about the threat they were trying to stop.

Roscoe's highlights of each day had been the morning meetings with Chairman Ray, Tacita, Fisher, Callie, and Maria. Each morning Fisher cooked them a wonderful breakfast and then after updating on progress and planning the first boarding, he and Maria did dishes.

He was starting to feel more and more attracted to her every day, and more comfortable with her.

And she clearly liked him as well and was flirting back with him. At some point, he hoped to spend a lot more time with her every day besides twenty minutes doing dishes.

It was finally, on the first day of the third week, that Fisher dropped a bombshell on the meeting.

"I think we can board the big ship in trans-tunnel flight."

The statement sort of hung there in the dining room air like a bad odor that no one wanted to comment on. Roscoe just couldn't even image anything like that being possible.

Chairman Ray smiled and motioned for Fisher to go on, then went back to finishing up his eggs.

"The ship's screens won't be active during trans-tunnel flight," Fisher said. "The ship is in the trans-tunnel for only about two hours, so it will be tight, but possible."

Maria shook her head and Roscoe didn't blame her.

"I didn't think it was possible to leave the confines of a ship in trans-tunnel flight," he said.

"It's not," Fisher said. "But we can attach my ship to the big ship near where we think a port is and then board after we come out of trans-tunnel flight. When it drops out, if our drives are off, it will take us out with it."

Again silence.

Tacita looked at Maria. "Chairman, has your team ascertained where the ports might be?"

"Yes," Maria said, nodding. "I believe that Chairman Fisher's option of attachment might not be necessary. We might be able to get the ship to open a port large enough for his ship to enter while in tunnel flight. The ship should have a very large landing deck if the design of this ship matches what we know of older Seeder designs."

"How about we scout this first?" Roscoe suggested, not liking at all what he was hearing. Far too many things could go completely wrong.

"How do you suggest we do that?" Fisher asked.

"You said the shields are off when in trans-tunnel flight?" Roscoe said.

"Scan it then," Maria said at the same time he did.

He smiled at her and her smile made it to her wonderful golden eyes just fine.

"Is that possible for you to do?" Chairman Ray asked Fisher and Callie. "It has been my understanding that scans in trans-tunnel flight are impossible at the moment."

Both Fisher and Callie looked at each other in silence for a moment, then Fisher turned to Chairman Ray. "They have been because no one has had a need until now to do that. Let us talk with our team and we'll have an answer to that in the morning."

Ray pushed his finished plate away and stood. Tacita did the same beside him.

"We are getting close," he said. "Good work, everyone."

With that they vanished.

Callie looked at Roscoe, smiling. "Great idea."

"If we can figure out how to make it work," Fisher said, staring at his wife clearly in deep thought.

"Go get to it," Roscoe said. "We'll handle the dishes and clean up."

"Thank you," Callie said, and an instant later they were gone.

Roscoe stood and started to gather up dishes, not really knowing what to say. For the first time he and Maria were really alone.

And suddenly he felt like he was back about four hundred years in school with a girl he liked and not knowing what to say.

She was gathering plates and cups and silverware on her side of the counter as well when he looked up at her.

She felt him staring at her and looked up, smiling at him with a twinkle in her golden eyes. "This time I'll wash."

He had no idea what that meant.

CHAPTER 9

Maria knew that both she and Roscoe had a lot to do, but she was in no hurry to leave and clearly he wasn't either.

She washed the dishes he gathered up and they talked about the mission. At one point he asked about her home planet and she told her about it, finishing with the fact that it had been a few hundred years since she had been back.

"That would be fun to see," he said. 'Sounds beautiful and cold."

"Cold describes it," she said.

Then she asked him where he was from and he described a standard seeded planet that had gotten into space a little ahead of others in the area. He had gotten a degree in astronomy and physics before joining his planet's military to get out into space. He had been recruited into the Seeders about ten years later.

"Two degrees?" she asked, looking at him, stunned.

"Only way I could get off the planet," he said, laughing.

The more she learned about this guy, the more she was liking.

After a far too short time period, they were done.

They both wiped down the counters last, talking about how great it would be to have a home base like this one.

"Tomorrow morning then," he said, smiling at her and holding her gaze.

She stepped up to him and kissed him for just an instant. Then she stepped back.

She could feel her breath short and she knew she was blushing, but she didn't care. It had been wonderful, even though she completely surprised him.

He also had the decency to be blushing as well.

"What was that, Chairman Boone?" he asked, smiling slightly.

"A promise for the future," she said, smiling back. "Until tomorrow."

And she transported back to her ship before she couldn't hold herself back and jumped him.

Or before he made a move to kiss her.

She had a hunch that neither of them would get anything done if that happened.

It took her a good half hour in the gym working off the excitement of being with Roscoe before she went back to a meeting with her team.

Two hours later they had worked out a computer generated list of a few million standard entrance codes that an old Seeder ship might use for its landing deck, if there was a landing deck.

They were all convinced there was, and that it would be large enough to hold just about any ship.

After that she had a small lunch and then went back to the gym to try to get Roscoe from her mind. Even a hard workout didn't do it.

It had been just too damned long since she had been with a man. And she had a hunch, the way she was feeling, she had never been with anyone like Roscoe.

Ever.

CHAPTER 10

The next morning at breakfast, Maria was cheerful and smiling. He had worried about her kiss and how she would react today.

All fine in that department. He had worried for nothing. She was as stunning and alluring as ever.

And even more friendly.

He had thought about her the entire day yesterday, trying to keep as busy as he could to cut down the time daydreaming of her.

It had worked a little, but not much. He pretty much had everything in place and ready to go.

About halfway through breakfast, Chairman Ray asked them about all their progress.

Maria told him how her crew had come up with a few million codes that might open the docking area if there was one like most Seeder ships. Then she said she and her crew were as ready as they ever would be.

Roscoe reported that *The Huntington* was ready and the other four warships were also in position and standing by. He was ready as well.

Callie and Fisher then reported that their team had figured out a way to get limited scans inside trans-tunnel flight, and had worked out exactly how to match the speed inside the trans-tunnel of the big ship.

The ship would only be in trans-tunnel flight for two hours starting tomorrow, then be in regular flight for fourteen days.

Fisher looked at Chairman Ray. "We're ready now if you want us to try to get a scan."

Chairman Ray nodded. Then he turned to Roscoe. "I want you and four of your best team on Chairman Fisher's ship."

Roscoe nodded, surprised, but it made sense in case something went wrong.

Ray turned to Maria. "I need you and four of your best scientists on the ship as well."

She nodded and said nothing, clearly understanding what Ray was doing.

Ray then turned to Fisher. "Only take the crew you need to get the scans. Leave all your data and most of your crew in one of the other science ships."

Fisher nodded as well. "We'll just need five also."

Roscoe was impressed. Chairman Ray had decided to move, but had reduced the risk down to painful, but not disastrous levels if something went wrong.

"We'll need to depart in one hour," Fisher said, "to be in position and at speed for the big ship's jump."

Roscoe nodded to Ray and stood. "Thanks once again for the great breakfast," he said to Fisher. "I'll be glad to do the dishes when we get back."

Ray laughed. "You all go. Tacita and I are not too old to do dishes."

"Thank you, dear," Tacita said, smiling at her husband.

They all laughed.

"My people will be ready and on board your ship in forty-five minutes," Maria said to Fisher.

Then she vanished.

"As will my people," Roscoe said.

Then he left, jumping back to his ship to get to Jonas and his command crew. He planned on taking the four of his top command crew, leaving *The Huntington* in the hands of Red and Mattie until they got back.

They were going to scan a very old and very advanced ship. There was going to be no telling what they would find or trigger.

And that had him both scared to death and excited at the same time.

CHAPTER 11

Maria liked working with Roscoe and felt comfortable with him. He and his top command crew were in a secondary control room on Fisher's small ship called *The Lady*.

His crew stood against the back bulkhead, armed and ready to go. The room was a high-ceilinged room that Fisher said had been used as an exercise room. He had converted it for this mission, along with other rooms.

His ship had a very comfortable feel and she had liked it the moment she stepped on board. The carpet in the hallways and rooms was soft, but not thick. Colors were tan and all chairs were form-fitting.

Fisher and Callie had decorated the hallway walls with various paintings and images from different planets. Often the images were changing, showing fantastic beauty from varied worlds. Maria bet that if she asked Fisher and Callie, each image and painting would have a story from the last three hundred years they had been together.

Fisher had said that most of the time the ship was on one of the big landing decks of his large Seeder research science ship. But he and Callie lived on this ship as their own personal apartment and always kept it at the top performance and with top equipment for all tasks.

Maria's crew stood near her on her right, watching the big image screen on the wall and the heads-up displays in front of Fisher's three crew members.

She and Roscoe stood side-by-side. At one point she had moved so that he almost touched her left arm. She wanted him a lot closer than that at some point.

They had talked a bit while boarding about how excited they were for the coming mission. Now, as they waited in the last few seconds, she shifted from foot to foot, but he stood rock still. How he could do that was impossible for her to grasp in this situation. This was too exciting to not move.

The large screen on the wall kept them all informed as to what Callie and Fisher were doing in the small ship's Command Center.

The big screen also showed the huge old Seeder ship flashing through space at near light speed.

The big Seeder ship was so large, no perspective was possible. It was impossible for her to grasp that someone had built something that big.

"Matching speed now," Fisher said.

She also found it hard to believe that this ship could move this fast. Nothing she knew of had near-light speed.

"Jump to trans-tunnel flight with the big ship in ten seconds," Callie reported.

"Here we go," Roscoe said, glancing at her and smiling.

She smiled at him. He seemed so cool under pressure situations. She wanted to just clutch something. She liked more and more about him, she had to admit. She forced herself to go back to watching the monitors. She couldn't let herself get distracted at this moment by his incredible looks and dark eyes. She was tempted to reach out and hold his hand, but she didn't.

"Two, one," Fisher said from the control room and the small ship jumped to trans-tunnel.

The stars streaked and everything on the screen went from clear to gray as it always did in fast trans-tunnel flight.

The big ship was right beside them, also in trans-tunnel flight.

Fisher had matched the jump perfectly. Amazing. She didn't know this was possible either, for two ships to be inside the same trans-tunnel flight.

Wow, Fisher and his team were really something.

"Ready for scans," Callie said.

In front of Maria, the three crew members from Fisher's team worked their boards quickly. On the big screen, and on the heads-up displays, was where they all hoped the scan results would start appearing.

"Nothing seeming to block the scans," Fisher reported from the Command Center.

Maria now wanted to jump up and down she was so excited. She was about to see inside a million-year-old Seeder ship. Beside her Roscoe didn't even move. He had some amazing control.

"Ready," Fisher said.

"Now," Callie said.

Nothing.

Screens showed the same image of the big ship in trans-tunnel flight.

Maria was disappointed for a moment, then suddenly everything changed.

The trans-tunnel streaks and grayness vanished.

And what appeared on the screen was something Maria couldn't comprehend in the slightest.

Fisher's ship now sat like a tiny dot on a vast plain of decking of some sort. Distant ceiling lights illuminated the vast space that looked like it could easily cover a large city.

The ceiling was so far overhead, it almost couldn't be seen.

"Oh, shit," Jonas said from behind her. "We triggered something."

Beside her, Roscoe snapped around. "Full alert. Jonas, to the control room."

Without looking around, Maria knew Roscoe's military crew snapped instantly into action, weapons at the ready as each took up a position near assigned members of the other two teams.

Roscoe had his pulse rifle off his shoulder and ready, standing beside her, his attention now on the screens as well as everyone in the room.

She glanced at him and then took a deep breath to calm herself and get back to thinking, just as Roscoe was doing.

"Seems we are inside the big ship," Fisher said from the control room, his voice sounding impossibly calm.

"It would seem that way," Maria said, shaking her head. Then she said to Fisher with more authority. "Can we get a signal out to Chairman Ray?"

A moment later Ray's face came on the screen.

She was never so happy to see a face in her life. She released the breath that she had been holding.

"We are inside the big ship," Fisher reported to Ray. "Our scans triggered a transport of some sort."

Ray just nodded. The man had ice in his veins just as Roscoe. "Everyone safe?"

"We are, and still scanning," Fisher said. "Transmitting data to you now as it comes in."

Ray glanced to his right for a moment, then nodded. "Continue as long as you can."

Maria was even more excited that Ray was getting their scans. That was a very, very good sign.

"I'm assuming," Fisher said, "that if we are still here when the ship drops out of trans-tunnel in an hour or so and goes behind its screens, our transmissions will be cut off."

"Understood," Ray said, nodding.

"Suggestions?" Fisher asked.

Ray stood silent for a moment, then shrugged slightly, his long gray hair bouncing on his shoulders. "Find a way to turn or stop that ship before it destroys those planets," Ray said.

"Understood," Fisher said.

Then Ray said simply into the camera. "Roscoe, take care of those people in there."

"Understand, Chairman," Roscoe said from beside her. "We will."

"Good luck," Ray said and cut off.

"Scanning data still pouring out and being received," Fisher said. "Chairman Mundy, Chairman Boone, meet me in the kitchen."

"Understood," Maria said.

Beside her Roscoe nodded and then followed her out of the

secondary Command Center and down the short hall toward the small ship's kitchen.

She was inside an ancient and more than likely very deadly Seeder ship.

A dream come true for her life's work.

And a nightmare at the same time.

SECTION TWO:

THE PAST CONTROLS

CHAPTER 12

Roscoe had been worried right from the start about their scans triggering a defense mechanism. They had prepared Fisher's ship with supplies and other needed items for just this contingency. And everyone on board had brought a week's worth of clothes that could be washed if needed. From the looks of it, Fisher's wash machine was going to get a workout before this was all settled.

But so far, nothing seemed deadly.

So far.

But he was going to take no chances that didn't need to be taken.

Fisher smiled at them as Roscoe and Maria arrived in the kitchen. Roscoe had his pulse rifle over his shoulder for the moment, but he could get to it quickly. His team was going to be close to any of the other team members at all times in case a group were transported out of Fisher's ship. He wanted one of his armed team with the others.

Roscoe glanced around at the kitchen. It could hold about six sitting around a nifty wooden dining table secured to the floor and the cooking area seemed state-of-the-art from what Roscoe could tell. He wasn't much of a cook, but he tried at times.

Roscoe could see a pantry stocked completely full just beyond one side of the kitchen. He knew that in other places on the ship there were enough supplies on board to feed the fifteen of them for a year, at least.

He sure hoped this mission didn't take that long, or a lot of people on those planets ahead of them were going to die.

Maria seemed calm now, not as excited as she had been before they jumped into trans-tunnel flight. Her excitement had been almost infectious and he loved that feeling of looking at the good things in something instead of always the bad. She balanced him well.

"This sure feels familiar," Fisher said, smiling, seemingly not at all concerned about the situation as he opened the fridge and offered them water or something else to drink.

Both Maria and Roscoe declined, so Fisher took out a bottle of a pink fluid and sat down at the kitchen table, indicating that they should join him.

"Familiar?" Maria asked as she sat across from Fisher. "How?"

Roscoe went over and leaned against a bulkhead near Maria, preferring to stand at the moment. It was going to take him some time to relax at this point.

Fisher took a drink and sighed. "When my friend and I first ran into a large ship coming to rescue the population of the planet where we have the lodge, our ship, this ship, in a much more primitive state, was teleported inside a huge landing deck. It was a smaller deck by a long ways from what we are in now, but still huge by our little ship's standards."

"Is it something about this ship that makes people want to do that?" Roscoe asked.

Fisher laughed and Maria shook her head and smiled at him, which he appreciated more than he wanted to admit. The tension in the room seemed to ease a lot from his joke question and he loved it when those golden eyes of hers looked fondly at him.

"Must be," Fisher said.

"What happened that first time?" Maria asked.

"Scared to death, we just went outside to introduce ourselves. Seeders, by their very nature, are a peace-loving group. We didn't know that at the time, but we do now."

Roscoe had to admit, that was true. But as Sector Justice forces knew so well, they still needed to know how to defend themselves. This huge ship clearly had good defenses.

"So are you suggesting we go introduce ourselves?" Maria said.

"Can you think of another option," Fisher asked, "after we study what we are getting from the scans, of course. They sure know we are here. I have nothing on this ship that could even pretend to block a scan, even if we wanted to."

Roscoe nodded at that. "How long until preliminary scans will be done?"

Fisher shrugged. "This ship we are in is bigger than many moons, so it's going to take some time to really cover it. But honestly, we'll know if we're alone and the focus of our mission in two hours."

"Can you feed the scans to my people in a place in the ship where we could work?" Maria asked.

Roscoe knew the answer, since he had checked out and helped Fisher set up the ship before the mission. But he let Fisher answer.

"We can," Fisher said. "We retrofitted our second exercise room with ten work and scanning stations before this mission."

He looked over at Roscoe. "I assume you are going to want to look at all the scans as well."

"I am," Roscoe said. "And my second-in-command, Jonas, will as well. We'll study monitors in the room with Chairman Boone's team. The rest of my team will remain on guard with each group in case a group is transported off the ship without warning."

"Very good thinking," Fisher said, nodding. "So in three hours, after the big ship drops back into real space, the three of us will meet here and decide how to proceed next."

Maria nodded and smiled at Roscoe as she stood. She patted him on the arm. "Let's go to work."

Roscoe could tell she was clearly back to being excited, and since the history of Seeders was her passion and life's work, he could certainly understand that.

His passion was to keep everyone safe. And he needed to know what was inside this monster old ship to even begin to do that.

And secondly, he needed to keep them all focused on one task: Stopping this ship before it killed millions of others on defenseless planets.

CHAPTER 13

The next three hours went by quickly, too fast, as far as Maria was concerned. The former exercise room turned second scanning room was long and fairly narrow. Fisher had set up ten stations down one wall. The other walls were covered in art and some of the exercise equipment had been pushed together in a back corner.

The floor was covered in a comfortable mat-like substance that felt soft and warm to her feet. It was a comfortable place to work, but she wouldn't have cared. She could have done this work standing in a closet and she wouldn't have cared.

The scans they were getting of the big ship were amazing.

It had become clear after the first hour that there was no one alive here, even though the ship had been designed for millions of humans to live comfortably for very long periods of time.

And she had a hunch that was a very, very low guess as to the number this ship could actually hold. She just couldn't imagine a ship holding more, so her brain stopped her there.

All of the scans from the three areas of the ship, the main scanning room, the control room, and this room, were being fed into a central image and slowly in that three-dimensional image, pieces of the ship were coming together.

Part of this ship was nothing more than a huge city, plain and simple, with housing that went from small apartments to five bedroom suites. It had what looked like schools, shopping, large areas that would be parks when planted, and so on.

The ship also carried a good five hundred other huge ships on one landing deck. All those ships were also empty of human life, but designed to hold thousands of humans per ship comfortably.

In fact, each ship was bigger than Chairman's Ray's ship, one of the biggest the Seeders had working right now in any of the Local Sector galaxies.

The big ship was also riddled with massive warehouse rooms stacked full of who knew what. Every warehouse looked completely untouched and her scans could not seem to tell what was in any of them. They were just too far away.

And from what she could tell, there were thousands of science labs and other areas for unknown reasons. Offices and work areas she guessed.

Roscoe was at the screen beside her, his rifle over his shoulder. She noticed he was amazingly good at running scans and comfortable on the heads-up board. He seemed to be focused on different areas of the ship than she was.

She liked having him that close and had stopped herself from excitedly showing him something at two different points. It seemed she just wanted to share things with him.

She had always been a loner by nature. This kind of desire to share and be close to another person was different for her and she honestly liked it more than she ever thought she would. And she had no idea why he was bringing that out in her. No other man she had known ever had.

Roscoe's second-in-command, Jonas, had focused his scanning on the Command Center for the big ship.

After three hours, Fisher came in and motioned for her and Roscoe to come talk with him in the kitchen again.

"We're going to need to feed people pretty soon," Fisher said as he entered the kitchen and took a container of water from the fridge and sat down. "We've set up a room as a dining hall and we have a meal already prepared and ready to just heat and serve when we call dinner. After this first meal, we're going to need to do more cooking."

Maria nodded, sitting down at the table across from Fisher again. Roscoe once again stayed standing and close to her.

"How about a group of one person from each team be in charge of a meal," she said, "and we rotate around."

She hadn't given a thought to eating, but knew they had to in order to keep everyone fresh. She also knew that Fisher's ship had been set up for enough sleeping quarters for all of them before the mission in case something like this might happen.

"I think we need to keep at least three people on the scans at all times," Roscoe said, "sort of as a guard. We can set up a rotation on that as well."

"Agree with both," Fisher said. "Even though all of us have been scanning for hours now, we still really don't know what's out there."

"I'm not really wrapping my mind around the size of this ship," Roscoe said. "I figured that if we set off walking from here to the Command Center, it would take us two weeks time if we covered about twenty kilometers per day."

Maria had done similar calculations. "I agree. I'm having trouble with the size as well. I did a calculation on a ten kilometer per day pace that it would take over a month simply to get from here to the other side of that huge hanger deck with all the large ships on it."

"So we can't be doing much walking," Fisher said. "The ship must have some sort of transport system like our big ships do."

"I think we're better off just transporting ourselves for the moment," Roscoe said. "Not sure how much we want to trigger into this ship's systems until we can get to that Command Center and see the path and the mission the ship is intended to accomplish."

Maria smiled at him. "I agree. In fact, I suggest we just stay here for the next forty-four hours until the ship drops back into trans-tunnel flight and we get information from Chairman Ray and his people. They will have had fourteen days to analyze what we sent them in those first two hours."

"I was going to suggest the same," Roscoe said, smiling at her. "Better we know where we are headed before we go wondering around and get lost in this huge ship."

"Any early theories as to what this ship is?" Fisher asked Maria.

She took a deep breath and for the first time since Chairman Ray had sent her the first data, she decided to mention her theory.

"I think this is a Seeder Mother Ship," she said.

"A what?" both Fisher and Roscoe asked at exactly the same time.

"There is one theory in history that Seeders have been seeding for more millions and millions of years than we can imagine," Maria said.

Roscoe and Fisher nodded.

Maria went on. "One theory is that a wave, a direction of seeding from galaxy to galaxy starts with a Mother Ship. Maybe this very ship has started many waves, then been restocked and sent ahead again. We don't know, or maybe this is a new ship, if one-point-four-millions years is new."

Roscoe sat back and looked at her, his dark eyes intense. Fisher was just looking puzzled.

"Remember," Maria said, "that I showed you the big spiral galaxy that I think this ship came from. And that our branch of Seeders left that galaxy and started off in this direction."

She could tell that Roscoe was starting to understand. In the short time they had been working together, she had come to realize he was really smart, maybe one of the smartest people she had ever met.

"They sent a wave of Seeder ships off toward here," Maria said, "then launched this ship so that it would meet the front wave, allow us to staff it and start off in a completely new direction as well as going to Andromeda."

"What made you think this?" Fisher asked.

"I've thought it right from the start," Maria said. "But it was only speculation. Now that I've seen early scans of the inside of this ship, I'm fairly sure."

"Why?" Roscoe asked, his dark eyes focused on her like she hoped they would be for a long time to come.

"That hanger deck full of ships, to start with," she said. "They are frontline seeder ships almost identical to the ones working Andromeda Galaxy right now."

Again both men nodded.

"Noticed that," Roscoe said.

"And because Seeders always just move to the next closest galaxy," she said, smiling at Roscoe's wonderful eyes as he intently stared at her. "And the closest galaxies were not in this direction from that huge spiral galaxy. In fact, taking this route to our Local Group of galaxies might be the third wave of Seeders that left that galaxy."

"Oh," Roscoe said, shaking his head.

"Do we Seeders ever do anything small?" Fisher asked.

"No, even my headache is large trying to grasp this," Roscoe said.

At that, Maria wanted to just stand and kiss him as she laughed. But somehow, she managed not to.

Barely.

CHAPTER 14

To Roscoe, spending that first night on Fisher's ship seemed almost like camping back when he was a kid on his home planet.

He could feel the pressure of the huge ship around him like he was in a deep forest a long ways from any city.

And he could really feel the responsibility of the safety of the fourteen people in the ship with him. So far nothing at all had seemed threatening, and the more they learned about the big ship, the more he doubted there was much to worry about as far as attack.

But even still, for the moment, he and his men had set up a rotating guard. And Maria and Fisher both had one of their people each stay on the scanning duty, running as many scans as possible continuously.

So at any given point, three of the twelve of them were awake.

He wasn't scheduled for a two-hour guard shift yet, but there was no chance that he could sleep. He normally didn't need much sleep, but he knew at some point he would have to get some. However, just lying there in the small room they had assigned him and staring at the ceiling wasn't going to work, and he knew himself enough to know that.

So, he took a shower, then changed clothes into a white t-shirt and comfortable slacks, then with his pulse rifle over his shoulder, he wandered back first to the dinner area and picked up a container of water and a piece of dark bread that had tasted fantastic and slightly sweet at dinner. Then he went down the wide hallway to the big scanning room.

Not only were the two there that had shifts, and Jonas standing against the wall near them on guard duty, but Maria was there, hunched forward, staring at something in her heads-up projection.

Obviously, she couldn't sleep either, although her red hair looked damp like she had also taken a shower, and she had on what looked like a form of cotton pajama bottoms with blue flowers and a sweatshirt and slippers of some sort.

Her red hair was pulled back tight and he could see the freckles on her neck.

She was unbelievably attractive, even hunched forward over a work station like that. He just wanted to go up and rub her shoulders and kiss her neck, but now was far, far from the time.

"Couldn't sleep either, huh?" he asked about halfway across the room after he nodded to Jonas.

She turned and smiled at him, her smile beaming, clearly glad to see him. He liked that a lot.

"Far too excited," she said. "Take a look at this."

She turned back to her board and the image floating in the air in front of her.

He stared for a moment, but couldn't make any sense of it. It seemed to be some sort of writing. "What am I looking at?"

"I think it's the name of this big ship," she said.

Her fingers were running over her board faster than he had ever seen anyone move. The freckles on her shoulders almost moving in a dance as her arms and hands flashed over the controls.

"I'm working on language programs," she said. "As with all human cultures, languages all have certain basics and when I hit on the right combination, I'll have the language. We've been loading language into our language program from around the big ship since the first scans. From signs on doors to warning signs in engineering to this."

"Will we then be able to internalize it," he asked, "so we can understand it when we read anything on this ship?"

She nodded. "Easily. Just as we do with any human culture, I can have all of us speaking and reading this ship's old language once we crack the pattern."

"Got it!" one of Fisher's people named Dan said from beside Maria. "Transferring it to you now."

"Wonderful," Maria said, almost jumping in her chair with excitement. Roscoe had to admit, it was impossible around her to not be excited.

"Got what?" Fisher asked as he came into the room, clearly also not able to sleep.

"Language," Maria said. "Dan cracked it."

Fisher came up behind his team member and gave him a congratulatory pat on the shoulder.

Then Maria clapped her hands and started laughing as she stared at the projection of the words.

"What's so funny?" Fisher asked a moment before Roscoe could.

"You folks want to know the name of the big ship we are sitting inside?"

"Very much so," Fisher said, smiling back at the infectious excitement from Maria.

"This ship is called *Morning Song*."

All Roscoe could do was shake his head.

A giant ship, that if not stopped, would destroy planets and kill billions, was named *Morning Song*.

He flat wasn't sure what to think of that.

CHAPTER 15

The first two days were nothing but one exciting discovery after another on the scans of the big ship. She hadn't slept much, but that didn't matter. This was the find of a dozen lifetimes and sleeping seemed to be an inconvenience.

And she loved spending time around Roscoe and he didn't seem to sleep much either. She loved his smile, his intense questioning eyes, and his dry sense of humor.

And he seemed to want to be around her as well, which pleased her more than she wanted to admit.

Now, all of her team and Roscoe and two of his team were in the big scanning room, waiting the last few minutes for the ship to jump to trans-tunnel flight. Fisher and Callie were back in the Command Center with a guard from Roscoe's team and the rest of Fisher's team were in the first scan center with another of Roscoe's team on guard with them.

She had no idea what was going to happen next. She hoped nothing but getting in contact with Chairman Ray.

In real time, Chairman Ray and his people had had fourteen days to go over those first scans. She hoped they had a lot more information. The possibility of that had her really excited.

But she could feel her stomach twisting in slight worry as well. No telling what would happen next when the ship jumped back to trans-tunnel drive. It might dump them back into space and not let them back inside.

Anything was possible.

"Ten seconds," Fisher said from the Command Center.

Maria glanced away from her screen and up at Roscoe's serious face. She was really starting to admire him and like him more than she wanted to admit. But right now he was focused and on guard, standing close to her. And she actually felt far safer with him close by.

That surprised her as well, but she liked it.

She had a scan running of the *Morning Song's* big Command Center to see if anything changed when the jump to trans-tunnel happened. She didn't expect to see anything, but she had decided to scan there even so.

"Two. One. Now," Fisher said.

After a few seconds of waiting, Fisher said, "Chairman Ray, do you copy?"

It took another moment before Chairman Ray's voice came back strong. "Strong and clear."

On a center screen in the room, Chairman Ray's smiling face appeared. He was clearly relieved and Maria could hear applause around him over the communications link.

Maria let out the breath she was holding. Beside her she could feel Roscoe relax and exhale as well.

"Sending data we have taken in the last two days on the *Morning Song*," Fisher said to Ray.

"Receiving," Ray said after a moment. "And you got the language figured out I see."

"We do, Chairman," Fisher said. "But we will need to access the big ship's command systems and other systems to figure out the *Morning Song's* mission. We will be doing that next unless your data bring up something we have not yet discovered."

Maria watched as Chairman Ray shook his head, his long gray hair moving on his shoulders as he did. "We have found, in searching carefully everything you sent us at first, no real threats from the ship itself."

"Besides getting lost," Fisher said.

Ray laughed. "There is that. That ship is impossible for most to comprehend the size."

"It is," Fisher said.

"So, I assume Chairman Mundy and Chairman Boone are on this link," Ray asked.

"Everyone on the ship is listening and on the link," Fisher said. "We seem to all be in the belly of this beast together."

Ray nodded. "Chairman Mundy," Ray asked Roscoe, "Do you see any obvious dangers in exploring?"

"Nothing, Chairman," Roscoe said, "after two days of scanning, it seems clear."

"Chairman Boone?" he asked.

"No dangers that my team has found, Chairman," Maria said, agreeing with Roscoe. In two days she and her team had found nothing that seemed even slightly dangerous.

Ray nodded, then asked Maria, "Do you think this is still a Seeder ship?"

"I do," Maria said, her stomach twisting in excitement. "I'm convinced this is a Seeder Mother Ship and the mission of this ship is to find a large crew and leave the Milky Way in a different direction from Andromeda and the path of the current leading edge of seeding that is going on in Andromeda."

Chairman Ray nodded. "We have come to that same conclusion."

Maria felt her heart race. These Mother Ships had only been a distant and faint myth of Seeders. Now she found herself inside one.

Then Chairman Ray's face became very serious. "We have exactly 161 days before the big ship plows into a populated system and takes out a moon and a number of other bases. We might be able to get those evacuated in time and have started that preparation now."

"Good," Roscoe said softly beside her.

Ray went on. "But the *Morning Song* plows into your home base world, Fisher and Callie, in 167 days and destroys it completely. We are mounting preparations for an emergency evacuation if it comes to that, but will only be able to get a few million out of the billion now on that world."

"We'll get it stopped, Chairman," Fisher said, and Maria found herself nodding in agreement.

"Your timeline is much shorter, you understand," Chairman Ray said.

"Twenty-two days and four hours," Fisher said. "We will stop it, turn it, or destroy it in that amount of time."

Maria again felt her stomach twist. This ship was the greatest treasure from the history of the Seeders. They had to stop it, she understood that, but if she had anything to say about it, they would do it without destroying it. They flat had to.

"Get started and dump data with each trans-tunnel flight," Chairman Ray said. "We'll do what we can in helping from this side."

"Thank you, Chairman," Fisher said.

"Good luck," Chairman Ray said and the screen went blank.

Maria did her best to just let herself breathe.

"Chairmen Boone and Mundy to the kitchen," Fisher said. "Five minutes."

Roscoe smiled at her as she stood. "Looks like we get to go exploring very soon."

At that she actually smiled, pushing back the ticking clock and letting the excitement of exploring an ancient ship the size of a large moon come forward.

"I love exploring new places," she said, smiling at him.

"Actually," he said, "so do I." Then he smiled and raised one eyebrow.

She wasn't at all sure what he meant exactly, but she liked the idea either way.

She laughed and said, "Why does that not surprise me."

CHAPTER 16

Roscoe knew there were two major points of danger for the crew. And about fifty million minor ones. But those he couldn't deal with. But he could take a few precautions on the major danger moments.

His first major point was when they first left Fisher's ship. If the big ship had a defense system, leaving the ship would be one place they all would stand no chance of any defense.

Of course, the big ship could have taken them off of Fisher's ship at any point, but it had not.

Their scans showed that when they had arrived, the big ship powered up all environmental systems. After two days, every room and area in the ship had breathable atmosphere and was heated. Even the warehouses.

But no other systems seemed to be running at all. And that told him they were going to have to turn them on.

Fisher's science team had informed him that the ship had maintained vacuum atmosphere interior and extremely cold temps before they arrived. Maria had confirmed that through her team.

So it seemed the ship was welcoming them by at least turning on the lights. Roscoe wasn't so sure if he liked that or not.

At least it allowed them to explore easily.

Maria and her people had also discovered that the ship had repair units that replicated and replaced any near-failing part during the long voyage. Some of those were on tasks now in various places in the ship.

Roscoe just found it all stunning.

So now, they had done all the scans they could. They had to step out of Fisher's ship and onto the decks of the big hanger.

He and Jonas were going to be the two to do it first.

And he had convinced Fisher they needed to do that one act while still in contact with Chairman Ray and send him all scans of the result.

So one hour after they had gotten in touch with Chairman Ray again, and with just under an hour left in trans-tunnel flight for the big ship, Jonas and Ray stood side-by-side, rifles over their shoulders, ready to go. They had decided to not seem threatening in any way, which was why they had their guns on their shoulders.

"See you in a moment," Roscoe said to Fisher and Maria.

She smiled, but he could see the worry in her eyes.

"I'll jump us," Roscoe said to Jonas, who nodded.

"Do your thing, boss," Jonas said.

The next moment Roscoe had them standing on the big deck about a hundred paces from Fisher's ship.

The air smelled sort of stale, but not bad, and had a slight chill to it.

Roscoe looked around, not sure what to expect.

The monster room around them was too large to grasp. Like a distant sky, the ceiling overhead seemed to be full of lights. To his right, Roscoe could see a wall of some sort, but he had no idea how far that was, or even how tall that wall might be.

Scale was totally lost in a space like this, so much so, it almost made him dizzy.

"Wow," Jonas said, slowly turning to look around. "Scans don't even come close to showing the immensity of this place."

"Any problems?" Chairman Ray asked, his voice clear to Roscoe.

Roscoe knew that about a thousand people were watching their every move and monitoring all data they were sending back from their sensors. Roscoe hadn't wanted them wearing helmets, so they had on communications links with implanted mikes and ear buds. And about three ways to track them if the ship took them somewhere else.

Anyone stepping onto this ship would have those communication methods and tracking devices.

Maria answered him. "All scans of the *Morning Song* are showing no alarms or activity at all."

"We ants out here on the big field see nothing either," Roscoe said, slowing turning and admiring the massive hanger deck.

"Seems the ship doesn't mind us," Maria said.

"Coming in," Roscoe said.

Roscoe jumped him and Jonas back to a special decontamination room on Fisher's ship and the two of them were scanned at levels Roscoe didn't want to think about.

"Clear on the decontamination," Fisher said.

"We agree from here," Chairman Ray said.

"A clean ship that has warmed up the place and turned on the lights," Fisher said.

"Seems we have some exploring to do," Roscoe said.

And after being out there in that huge space, that idea actually excited him for the first time.

CHAPTER 17

O ne hour after the big ship dropped back out of trans-tunnel flight and they lost communications with Chairman Ray because of the ship's shields, Maria found herself sitting beside Roscoe in the kitchen of Fisher's ship.

He had on a tight black shirt and black slacks with the same wide belt buckle he always wore. His long brown hair was pulled tight behind his head. For the first time since they had been inside the big ship, he had no rifle with him.

She wanted to just touch the muscles that were clear under the tight black shirt, but she didn't. Instead she let her leg sort of rest casually against his under the table. Being this close to him made her feel so much better in so many ways she wasn't sure she understood just yet.

Fisher and Callie were both there as well. All of them were sipping on containers of water and she had one in front of her as well, but hadn't touched it. Besides sitting so close to Roscoe, she was so excited about going out and exploring *Morning Song*, she almost couldn't sit still.

Fisher looked at her. "Do you have opinions of the most important areas to explore first?"

"Command Center, of course," Maria said. "We need to get control of this ship in some fashion or another and that has to be priority."

Beside her, she could see Roscoe nodding in agreement.

Fisher looked around at his wife, then back at Maria. "You won't get any disagreement on that at all. Second most important?"

Maria just shook her head. She wanted to see the entire ship, but she knew they had to prioritize right now. "Engines, then secondary control rooms, then living areas, then those big ships on that docking bay. We really need to see how they are outfitted and if they can function after all this time. On second thought, those should be right after the engine room."

Fisher looked at Roscoe. "Your list?"

Roscoe looked at Maria. "I can't disagree with that list at all."

Callie agreed and so did Fisher.

"So there are fifteen of us," Fisher said. "How would you suggest we split up or should we?"

Maria looked at Roscoe who nodded for her to go ahead.

"My suggestion," Maria said. "One from each team remain here on the ship running scans ahead of the three groups that are out. Three groups out at a time, four members in each exploring group. We need at least one member from each of our teams in each group."

"That feels right," Roscoe said.

Fisher turned to his wife. "Would you mind remaining on board this first time? I need someone in command here who knows how to fly *The Lady*."

"I was going to suggest that," she said.

Fisher turned to Maria again. "Who on your team knows the most about the Command Centers of older Seeder ships?"

"Hudson," she said, without hesitation.

Hudson was one of her youngest at three hundred years, but looked far older than he should because of his long black beard and shaggy hair. He had made it his passion to study and fly in reality and in simulations all old Seeder ships she could get him near. He could take apart old Command Centers with his eyes closed.

"So the three of us and Hudson head to the Command Center," Fisher said.

"Jonas could take a team to engineering," Roscoe said. "His passion is engines of all types."

Fisher nodded. "Two of my team are engineers as well. Perfect."

They spent the next half hour detailing out who would go first and so on. They decided that Maria had been right and the third most important place to explore was the big ships on the hanger deck.

Then there was nothing else to talk about.

Maria was almost floating off the deck as she headed for her cabin to get what she might need in the Command Center of the *Morning Sun*. This was all a dream come true.

But in the back of her mind, something was nagging at her. She felt completely home inside the *Morning Song*. Completely, and that felt both good and worried her. She had no idea where the feeling was coming from.

But in her excitement, she decided to just think about that later. Right now she got to explore a Seeder ship that was so ancient, she couldn't believe it actually existed.

And she was going to get to explore it with a man of her dreams.

It didn't get better than that.

CHAPTER 18

R oscoe had learned very early on that when something was going smoothly, something ugly was about to happen. It didn't always work that way, but his voice was telling him that was the case this time.

This ship had made him feel like an ant crawling somewhere on a planet's continent. The builders of this ship were far, far beyond the knowledge and years of the Seeders now or ones working Andromeda.

Sure, the ship had been built by humans. Seeders. But not humans like them at all. Humans far, far advanced. So why did ants like him think they could get control of something this big?

That thought just kept nagging him and he had no idea what to do about that at all.

And he felt completely at home on the big ship at the same time and that feeling worried him even more and kept him even more on guard.

He had insisted that each group only jump with line-of-sight as much as possible. That way the ship would be able to know they were coming and they wouldn't trigger alarms without warning.

He hoped.

"Ready?" he asked the three standing around him in the big former exercise room with the scanning stations. This room would be their jump base. Jonas's group had the main scanning room, and the third group was using a back open area in the dining room.

Fisher, Maria, and Hudson all nodded as one that they were ready. Maria's excitement for the moment had turned to serious worry. He wanted to hug her and tell it would be all right, but damned if he knew it would be.

"I'm going to do the jumping. I'll take us about a kilometer away across the deck along the path toward the Command Center."

Again they all nodded.

So he jumped them.

The incredible open space of the huge deck surrounded them.

The air did smell slightly stale this second time out, and the temperature was slightly under what Fisher kept his ship, but not too cold to be a worry.

Fisher's ship looked like a tiny toy sitting in the middle of a huge room from this distance.

"Stunning," Hudson said softly as if whispering wouldn't draw attention to them.

Roscoe turned to Maria who was slowly turning, trying to take it all in, her large golden eyes even wider than normal.

"How do we look out ahead?" Roscoe asked her after giving her a moment to be shocked and look around.

He then moved over next to her as she fumbled to get her scanner out. Her scanner gave him a clear image of where they were jumping to, and a clear path to the Command Center.

It was going to take him about thirty minutes of quick jumps to get them there, mostly down huge hallways that appeared to be the width of a two-lane highway and up through decks into more hallways.

She checked the scan and then showed it to him, her shoulder brushing his arm. "We're clear."

He jumped them again.

"Scans are clear," Maria said.

"Triggering nothing," Callie's voice came across clear in their ears. The three back on the ship were there to scan ahead and make sure no team triggered anything. "Second team leaving the ship."

"Understood," Roscoe said as they looked around.

He had jumped them right into the middle of one of the huge hall-ways. Fifty people could walk side-by-side in this hallway and not even touch shoulders. And the ceiling was high and the lights were hidden, but clearly there.

Hudson kneeled and touched the carpet under their feet. "I don't think this is fabric," he said. "I think it's the decking surface itself formed to be soft and slightly flexible."

Fisher pointed to regularly spaced panels about every twenty paces. The panels were dark. "Seems like they might have a ship-wide trans-port system like our own."

"Ours is like this one," Maria said, smiling. "This ship has been in flight since before Seeders came into the Local Group."

"Yeah, that," Fisher said, smiling back at her.

"Amazing," Roscoe said. "But glad we're not hiking. What are these rooms around us?" He pointed at the closed doors that lined the hall every fifty feet or so and seemed to blend perfectly into the wall.

"Offices of some sort," Maria said, looking at her scanner.

"So how are we on the path ahead?" Roscoe asked Maria, moving over again to stand beside her and look at her scanner.

"Clear," she said.

He nodded. "I'm going to pick up speed now until we get near the Command Center. We jump, check scan, and jump again. So stay close to me."

Twelve jumps through identical hallways later, they were sixty-five decks higher in the big ship and in the hallway outside the *Morning Song's* big Command Center.

So far, so good.

And that worried Roscoe far more than he wanted to admit.

CHAPTER 19

M aria stood one hundred paces from the big door that led into the Morning Song's Command Center. She couldn't decide if she was more afraid or excited. Both emotions seemed to be warring with each other.

Roscoe seemed very worried, but he didn't say anything. Fisher also looked worried and Hudson just looked excited.

"This is where we discover just how friendly this ship really is," Roscoe said.

"Callie?" Fisher asked into the air, "any signs of anything coming to life around us or in the Command Center?"

"Nothing," Callie said.

Maria studied her scans. It just showed the big room, nothing more. "Clear here as well," she said.

Roscoe nodded and handed Fisher his rifle. Fisher nodded and put it over his shoulder.

"Back in a moment," Roscoe said, striding down the hallway toward the big door. "Stay there."

Maria held her breath, watching him walk. More than likely he was scared to death, but he didn't show it in the slightest. He was more amazing than she had even known.

She didn't know what she expected when he approached the door, but nothing didn't seem possible. Yet that was exactly what happened.

Nothing.

He walked right up to the door and stopped.

The door didn't slide open. She watched as he looked around for a way to have the door slide open, but clearly he didn't find anything. So he looked back at them and shrugged.

And then vanished.

Clearly he had transported somewhere. Inside the control room, she hoped.

A few seconds later he was back beside her and she actually was so glad to see him, she reached out and grabbed his arm.

"Did I trigger anything?" he asked.

"Nothing," Callie said.

Maria checked her scanner as well, as did Hudson.

"Nothing," she said.

"Callie, watch us closely," Roscoe said.

"Understood," Callie's voice came back strong.

Roscoe jumped them inside the Command Center, just inside the door.

And the sight took Maria's breath away.

Just as with everything on this ship, the Command Center was huge. It had the classic three levels, with a good thirty stations and chairs around the top half-circle level, most facing the wall back, some facing the monster screen on the front wall that was massive.

The air smelled faintly of fresh roses and the floor was a light tan color and soft.

The second level had ten chairs on it, all facing the big front screen. All clearly had heads-up displays that were powered down at the moment.

And in the very center, slightly ahead of all the other stations, two huge chairs towered over any person that might be sitting in them. They were a soft white and dominated the center of the room. They seemed to be linked, form-molded out of one piece of material.

Everything in the room was a brown tone except those two huge molded chairs. The white made them stand out and gave them even more importance.

As Maria moved around the room, she could see that one-half of the two huge chairs was clearly labeled for a man, one for a woman. And between the two chairs was a natural place for the two people to hold hands molded into the chairs.

"You have triggered nothing," Callie said. "But having you in that room clearly gives some perspective to the size of the room on the scans."

"It's huge and amazing," Fisher said.

Maria was just too stunned to say anything. With Roscoe at her side, she slowly moved down and stood in front of the two big command chairs.

Finally Roscoe glanced at her. "Anything like this in the history of the Seeders?"

She slowly shook her head. "Nothing that I have found."

Nothing in anything she knew had prepared her for the sight of those two locked command chairs.

They simply took her breath away.

CHAPTER 20

They spent a good half hour exploring the large room without touching anything before Roscoe recovered enough to ask the question that bothered him a lot.

"Why aren't these stations powering up?" Without the control stations powered up and the big screen working in front of them and all the other wall screens working as well, a Command Center was just sort of a plain room.

And those two molded-together command chairs made no sense at all.

Both Hudson and Maria shrugged that they had no answer, which bothered him more than he wanted to admit.

"We're going to need to touch a panel," Fisher said. "Just see what happens."

Roscoe agreed and hated that idea, but the only hope they had of this ship getting under their control was to do just that.

He moved over to a panel closest to him on an upper deck station and touched it.

It did nothing for a moment, then a screen came up with ancient Seeder writing on it.

"Maria. Hudson," he said softly, but clear enough for them to hear.

Both of them scrambled to his side. Fisher was right with them.

"Does that say what I think it says?"

"Oh, shit," Maria said, staring at the screen.

"We need a damned password," Hudson said. "Are you kidding me?"

On the screen the clear letters that Roscoe could read thanks to Fisher and Maria's people cracking the language problem.

Welcome to the Morning Song.

Please enter command permission code.

After a moment the screen went dark.

"What happened?" Callie asked from the ship. "Scans show a tiny energy signature and then nothing."

"We touched a panel," Fisher said as Roscoe turned away. "We need a command permission code to take control of the ship."

"Oh," was all Callie said.

Roscoe looked at Maria who was standing staring at the big blank screen on the front wall.

He moved over beside her. "How can the Seeders expect us to know a command code after a million plus years? They clearly do."

"I honestly don't know," she said, her voice soft.

He looked around at the stunned look on Fisher's face. Hudson had dropped to the floor, sitting cross-legged with his head in his hands.

"I'm jumping us back to the ship to get some food," Roscoe said. "We can work there on this."

Maria nodded and a moment later he had them back in the slightly warmer and far more comfortable interior of Fisher's ship in the scanning room.

"Come on," Roscoe said, taking off his gear and stashing it near a wall and then helping Maria out of her pack and taking the scanner from her hands and putting her stuff next to his. "It's our turn to cook."

Fisher nodded. "I'll talk with Callie for a few minutes and join you both."

"I'm just going to sit here for a while," Hudson said, dropping into a chair at a screen.

With that, Roscoe took Maria's hand in his and led her slowly out of the big scanning room and down the small hallway toward the kitchen.

He loved the feel of her hand in his. It felt right and very natural.

She gripped his hand tightly, like he was saving her.

When they finally reached the kitchen, she let go of his hand and then faced him. "Thank you."

Before he could ask for what, she kissed him for the second time, and for the second time caught him by surprise.

But this time he kissed her back.

It was wonderful and they fit together. Her lips were firm and her body felt wonderful pressed against his.

The kiss lasted far, far too short a time before they broke apart and smiled at each other.

"That was great," he said. "Another promise for the future, I hope."

"A very near future," she said, smiling at him.

Then side-by-side, they went to work preparing dinner for fifteen people.

That felt wonderful.

And wonderfully natural to Roscoe.

Pretty soon they were both laughing.

He had a hunch that if they kept working together, they could solve even losing a million-year-old-password to control a machine that was about to kill millions.

CHAPTER 21

For the rest of the day and all the next day, teams jumped all over the *Morning Song* exploring everything they could in that short amount of time. Maria spent almost as much time out exploring than back in Fisher's ship.

And all the time Roscoe was at her side. He wasn't leaving it, but he was letting her decide where they go. He knew that she needed to work and didn't push her at all.

All teams reported back the same thing with every mission. All systems except environmental were dead on the big ship, waiting for someone to enter a command code.

And Maria felt like it was her problem, her mistake, that she didn't know the command code. After all, she was the expert on the history of the Seeders.

They had fourteen hours remaining until the big ship again jumped to trans-tunnel flight and they could contact Chairman Ray.

She was feeling more and more exhausted and discouraged, but about to jump out again after a light dinner when Roscoe took her by the hand.

"We need to rest."

She looked up into worried intense eyes of a man she had come to respect a great deal. And one she was more attracted to than she could ever imagine.

"We've been going now for twenty-nine hours," he said. "A few hours sleep might help get the answer to this."

She nodded. She had known she was getting tired, but hadn't realized it had been that long.

Hudson, who had come into the room at that moment and heard the last part of the conversation said, "Oh, thank the heavens. I'll be in my room sleeping if you need me."

"Seven hours," Roscoe said as Hudson turned and left.

Maria laughed. "Guess we do need to rest."

Roscoe tapped the communication link with Fisher. "We're resting the team for about seven hours."

"Copy that," Fisher said. "Thanks."

Roscoe took Maria's hand and led her down the hall to her room. "We'll meet in the breakfast area in seven hours."

She yawned and nodded, then looked up at him, smiling. "Not going to kiss a girl goodnight at the door?"

Part of her really wanted the sleep, part of her wanted him to kiss her and make her forget everything.

He smiled back and kissed her lightly. Then pulled back.

"Sleep," he said.

She pretended to salute and then turned and went into her room, closing the door behind her on a man she really wanted to have join her. How silly was that?

She put on her comfortable night cotton pants, a light t-shirt, washed her face and dropped onto her bed.

Three hours later she woke up. Screw it. She wanted to sleep with Roscoe, even if they might not sleep the entire time.

She slipped on her slippers and went out into the hallway and down two doors to his room. She opened it slowly and stepped inside.

He was snoring lightly on his side, facing the wall.

She crawled in behind him, put her arms around him and snuggled close. He smelled wonderful, like a fresh forest, and he felt even better. He was only wearing boxer shorts and his strong muscles and smooth skin felt fantastic under her arms and hands.

He stirred and she said softly. "Sleep."

He reached around and put a hand on her butt and pulled her even closer to his back. Then he said softly, "This is nice."

"Sleep," she said.

He nodded and a moment later he was back asleep.

In all her long life, she had never felt so comfortable and safe with another person in her bed.

How was this even possible?

And before she could even think about that question, she was asleep again.

CHAPTER 22

Roscoe awoke slowly, enjoying the feel of Maria pressed against his side. He was on his back and his arm was curled around her. She was snuggled up against him, her red hair fanned over his arm.

She smelled of a light maple syrup and her skin under his hand was stunningly smooth and her muscles were firm. He knew she worked out, but he had no idea she was in such good shape.

He managed to turn his head enough to not wake her to see the time on a small dresser beside the bed. It was an hour before they needed to be showered, have some breakfast and make another few jumps before *Morning Song* jumped to trans-tunnel and they could talk to Chairman Ray again.

"You awake?" she asked softly, her voice husky as he turned back.

"Starting to," he said.

"This is nice," she said, snuggling against him. "You sleep all right?"

"Wonderfully," he said, "except for this red-headed pixie waking me up sneaking into my room. Nothing but a great dream I'm sure."

She laughed and ran her hand back and forth over his chest. She then tipped her head up and kissed him.

And that kiss was one he would remember for a very long time. Slow, but intense.

Finally she pulled away and snuggled back with him again. "How much time do we have before we meet the team?"

"Not much," he said. "Time to take showers and get something to eat."

"Seriously?" she asked. "I haven't slept that long in years."

She pushed herself up and sort of half-crawled on top of his chest to see the clock beside his bed. "Damn," she said. "We're going to have to be quick and quiet then."

With that, she crawled completely on top of him and pulled off her t-shirt. Her breasts were perfect and firm, with dark pink nipples. The upper half of her chest was completely covered with freckles.

Then she stood up, one leg on each side of him, balancing herself on the bed.

She pushed down her pants and slipped them off, one leg at a time until she was standing over him, straddling him, totally naked.

"Wow," was all he could manage to say. It had been a long time since he had been with a woman and he could never, in all the decades, ever remember someone as open as she was about being naked.

Staring up at her would be an image he would never, ever forget for as long as he lived.

"Don't move," he said.

He quickly sat up and kissed her crotch softly as he kicked off first the sheet over him and then his shorts.

She looked at him and how excited he was and smiled down at him. "We need to be quick and silent."

"After looking up at this wonderful sight," he said, stroking her wonderful body, "quick won't be an issue. Silent on the other hand..."

She came down on him, spreading out over him and kissing him hard, holding his penis between her legs.

Then she sat up slightly and slipped him inside her.

"Yeah, silent is going to be a problem," she said.

Then, as she started to move on him, she smothered him in the most wonderful kiss he could ever remember.

And somehow, that long and intense kiss kept them from being too noisy.

At least he hoped it did.

He honestly didn't care.

CHAPTER 23

Fisher was cooking breakfast for him and Callie and Hudson when Maria and Roscoe walked in. She was holding his hand and she didn't care who saw it. It felt right and perfect. In all her life, she never thought that walking with a man holding hands would be something she would ever do, but they had walked from her room to the kitchen that way and she wanted to keep going.

The room smelled like cooking eggs and toast and made her stomach rumble.

Their quick lovemaking had been fantastic, and now they were both showered and refreshed. She had wanted them to take a shower together, but Roscoe rightly told her that if they did that, they wouldn't be on time.

But he made her promise him a shower check, like a rain check, only inside, just as wet, and a lot more fun.

She had laughed all the way through her own shower at that.

"You two manage to get some sleep?" Fisher asked without looking up from the stove.

Callie smiled and covered her mouth.

Maria let go of Roscoe's hand and sat down at the dining table.

"Refreshed and ready to go," she said, winking at Callie, who damn near burst out laughing.

Hudson had his attention buried in a portable scanner and seemed very intent and didn't notice a thing.

Roscoe just shook his head at her and smiled. Then he said to Fisher, "Wow, does that smell amazing."

"Two more minutes is all," Fisher said. "Your timing is perfect."

"What are you looking at?" Maria asked Hudson.

The unshaven man looked up at her and blinked. Clearly he had showered and gotten a little sleep, but if she knew Hudson, it hadn't been much. His full head of black hair and full beard was as much of a mess as she had ever seen it.

"I've been researching into every myth and history we have about Seeder Mother Ships," Hudson said. "I've found two references to the dual command chairs."

Maria almost went across the table at that. She had never found a one.

Even Fisher turned from the stove at that statement, but then went right back to tending to breakfast.

"What are they?" she asked. "Did you find out their purpose?"

"They are referenced as 'The chairs of knowledge' both times," Hudson said, doing air quotes around the chairs of knowledge part. "The myths say that the reason they are joint command chairs is because the human race can't exist without both men and women."

"Symbols," Callie said, nodding. "A Mother Ship like this one takes a joint command."

Maria looked at Roscoe. Then back to Hudson. "Chairs of knowledge?"

Hudson nodded. "Both references. All I can find so far."

"And from what we can tell," Fisher said, "every screen and system on the ship needs the command code password to activate. But it seems everything on the ship is also hooked in a fashion to the Command Center and in a way to those two chairs."

"After breakfast we jump back to the Command Center," Maria said, nodding and looking at Roscoe. "I think we may have just solved the command code problem."

"And what's that," Fisher said.

"Roscoe and I have to sit in those chairs."

She looked at Roscoe, who nodded, clearly agreeing.

"Oh, yeah, good idea," Hudson said, shaking his head in disgust.

"Do you think anything will happen?" Callie asked.

"More than likely it will just ask for the command code," Maria said. "But those chairs might be set to sense Seeders and descendants of the Seeders sent in this direction."

"So you are saying," Roscoe asked, "that this ship needs a way beyond basic scanning to tell we are descendants?"

"I think so," Maria said. "But I don't think we have anything to lose. And right now we need to take a few chances."

Roscoe nodded. "After breakfast we'll give it a try."

She smiled at him and wanted to kiss him, but right at that moment Fisher started serving wonderful-smelling eggs and perfectly browned pancakes and light toast made out of that wonderful sweet bread.

After the long night's sleep and the wonderful session with Roscoe, she was hungry.

And once again excited about exploring this incredible huge ship. They would figure out a way to stop it from hurting anyone.

She believed that now.

CHAPTER 24

Roscoe wasn't very fond of the idea of them sitting in those two big command chairs. But if Maria thought it might be the solution to getting control of this monster ship, he would do it with her. As she had said, time was clicking down and they had to take some chances.

He doubted much would happen when they sat down, but who actually knew.

Clearly, the chairs were designed for two people. And he certainly wasn't going to stand to one side and let her sit in those chairs with anyone else.

After breakfast, the four of them gathered in the scanning room that was their base. Roscoe made sure all four of them had the supplies they were going to need, then looked at Maria. "Ready?"

She smiled that wonderful smile of hers that reached her golden eyes and said, "As I'll ever be."

Fisher and Hudson both nodded, so Roscoe jumped them all to the Command Center.

They stored their gear against a wall next to the door that wouldn't open, then all four of them moved down in front of the two big command chairs.

They were clearly molded to fit a human body, not just something to sit in, but something that allowed the head to rest back like a half helmet, and the arms to rest partially surrounded by the material of the chair.

Hudson and Maria both took scans.

"As dead as everything on this ship," Hudson said.

Roscoe knew that if they hesitated at all, they might not try this. They had to get this idea out of the way before they could move forward.

He reached over and took Maria's hand.

She smiled at him and nodded.

"Callie, keep a sharp eye for any changes," Fisher said to his wife back in their ship.

Roscoe knew that Callie and two others would be watching every detail of the equipment around them.

"Together?" Maria asked Roscoe.

"Together," he said.

Then holding hands as the form of the two chairs showed, they sat down and scooted back into the tall white chairs.

Roscoe could feel the softness of the chair as it seemed to mold to his body.

"Anything?" he asked Maria, not wanting to turn his head to look at her.

In front of them both Fisher and Hudson had worried looks on their faces. Fisher was watching them while Hudson stared at his scanner.

"Nothing yet," Maria said. "But it's sure comfortable. I think it's moving and fitting to my form."

Roscoe could feel the chair finish adjusting and supporting him.

"Mine as well," Roscoe said.

Then suddenly everything changed.

Everything.

A blue translucent display screen appeared in front of him and Maria, between them and Fisher and Hudson. He could still see them through it.

And Roscoe could feel far more going on. He could feel his awareness expanding.

It was as if he could suddenly see everything about the ship.

And understand it all.

He could feel the connections in the ship to this chair.

And most importantly, he could sense and feel Maria beyond her hand he was holding.

She had become just sort of part of him. He couldn't read her thoughts exactly, but he could sense how she was thinking and feeling and her excitement about what was happening.

He was sort of blended with her. He had no other way to put it.

And he knew she was blended with him as well.

"This is kind of strange," he said softly.

"Very," she said. "But it feels right."

"Very right," he said.

He suddenly realized he wasn't afraid or on guard at all. This did feel right.

Almost being blended with Maria's mind felt natural as well. He wanted to know what she was feeling, have her beside him at all times.

"Odd," she said out loud. "I like this."

She had been almost thinking the same thing he had been thinking.

"Any idea what's going on?" he asked.

On the other side of the blue screen, Hudson said, "The entire ship has activity."

Maria squeezed Roscoe's hand and said, "Look at the screen."

The message on the screen was clear.

Welcome Chairmen.

The command code for Morning Song *is Sunrise.*

"Thank you, *Morning Song*," Maria said.

The first message faded and a second message appeared.

You are welcome.

. . .

Roscoe could feel himself being drawn down into understanding areas of the ship that he had no idea even existed. The ship was teaching him in a much more advanced way than language was taught to Seeders when they first came into the organization.

He was learning and understanding and completely comprehending what he was learning.

All in seconds.

"Shall we get the ship stopped?" he asked.

"What?" Fisher asked from the other side of the blue screen that he and Hudson clearly couldn't see.

He could sense Maria turn her attention back from learning.

"It's our ship now," she said.

He knew instantly that was true. *Morning Song* was their ship, jointly. "Let's get it stopped and repaired from its long journey."

"Perfect," Maria said.

Fisher stepped toward them. "Can we ask what you two are talking about?"

Roscoe looked through the blue screen at Fisher. "Get every member of our team here quickly. No need to leave anyone on your ship. We need them here."

"To do what?" Fisher asked.

"We need to get this ship stopped," Roscoe said.

"Oh," was all Fisher said.

As Roscoe and Maria waited, together, holding hands between the chairs and in their minds, they learned about their new ship, every detail of their new ship.

And so much more about each other.

CHAPTER 25

Maria couldn't believe the freedom and the lightness she felt sitting with Roscoe in the big chairs of knowledge. Now she understood why the legends called these chairs by that name.

Seemingly instantly, she knew Roscoe, knew his life, his dreams, his immense intelligence. And more importantly, she knew that he truly cared about people and loved being a Seeder.

She couldn't read his mind, but she sensed it all and knew what was right.

And she knew how much he cared for her, far more than she could have hoped, because she cared for him in the same way.

They were blended sitting in the big chairs.

Still individuals, yet blended as a team, working as a team.

It felt amazing to her. Just amazing.

And they were quickly learning every detail of the massive ship, from how the engines worked to the shields to the labs to the hanger bays. In her mind, she could see clearly Fisher's small ship sitting like a tiny bump in the big landing bay.

And she could even see the problem as to why the braking program hadn't kicked in and why the ship was still at full speed. It would be an easy fix, she knew that.

Her and Roscoe's eyes could see every detail, every room, every closet, of this wonderful big ship.

Through the ship's sensors, she could see the big Seeder fleet waiting for them at a point where the *Morning Song* would jump to trans-tunnel drive.

She even understood the physics now of trans-tunnel drive. Before, that had always baffled her.

And she knew that the intelligence that was *Morning Song* was very much an entity, a complete life in its own way that had kept this ship alive and moving and repaired as much as possible through a voyage in deep space of one-point-four million years.

Now, as their teams gathered around them in the big Command Center, Roscoe took charge of assigning each a station in the big room.

"Command code is Sunrise at each station," he said as they quickly moved to their stations.

"Put in the command code," Maria said, "and then put your right hand beside the image where indicated."

"What will that do?" Fisher asked as he moved to a position beside Roscoe on his right.

Callie moved to a position on the left of Maria.

"*Morning Song* will give you a quick training in the station's use," Roscoe said.

"Perfectly safe," Maria said.

He squeezed her hand and as they felt each of their friends come on line and spend a moment learning the station, she and Roscoe kept learning, taking in every detail of the big ship.

Before she could not imagine the scale of the ship. Now it all seemed clear and logical and useful.

"Notice we have no mission statement or history," Roscoe said as they waited the few moments it was taking for everyone to get trained.

"I did," she said.

On the screen in front of them, *Morning Song* replied to his statement.

· · ·

That information will be supplied after you have control
   of Morning Song and have all safe.
   Your training will take some time.

"Thank you again, *Morning Song*," Maria said.
   Again the first message faded and a second message appeared.

You are again welcome.

"Everyone is now on task," Roscoe said a moment after Maria sensed that the stations in the big room were manned and functioning.
   "Please monitor your stations carefully," Maria said. "Big screen is coming up."
   The entire wall beyond their thin blue monitoring screen became a screen showing space ahead of *Morning Song*.
   Then Maria had the blue monitoring screen lowered and both her and Roscoe's heads-up displays appeared.
   They were still holding hands, but Maria and Roscoe both knew that would not bother them in the slightest. In fact, it was critical to them staying in contact and working as a unit. All of their commands and actions would be through either *Morning Song* or the crew around them.
   "We're going to flip *Morning Song* 180 degrees," Roscoe said. "Fisher, stay with me on this. Everyone, monitor your stations. Shout if the slightest thing gets out of line."
   "Understood," Fisher said.
   "*Morning Song*," Roscoe asked. "You understand what is needed?"

Yes.

Maria said, "Callie, please contact Chairman Ray. Tell him we are in control of *Morning Song* and to have all ships stay out of the way until we are finished. Link him into the monitors in here, but please do not put through his audio. Tell him of that restriction so he won't worry."

"Understood," Callie said.

Maria watched and monitored everything closely as Roscoe and *Morning Song* took the big ship and eased her over so that her engines were now facing in the direction of flight. *Morning Song* itself did most of the maneuver, but it could not have done it without Roscoe's mind and skill as a pilot.

Maria could see Fisher watching closely from his station.

Maria knew that this wonderful ship had taken almost four hundred years to climb to this rate of speed. Now they had to slow it much, much faster if they had any hope of saving millions of lives.

Any hope at all.

"We'll get it done," Roscoe said, clearly sensing her worry.

But they both knew that the *Morning Song* was not meant for such intense braking. They would not have it stopped before they plowed into Fisher and Callie's home world.

But they had other options.

CHAPTER 26

"Complete," Fisher said. "Engines are now facing in the direction of travel."

"Engines coming on line," Maria said.

"Bring the engines up to full power slowly," Roscoe said. "Everyone, monitor your stations closely. Take your time."

Roscoe couldn't believe that he and the intelligence that was *Morning Song* had just done a very difficult maneuver. He had always considered himself a good pilot, but flying this ship would have been far beyond him. You don't just flip a ship the size of a moon 180 degrees with chances of tearing it apart.

Maria squeezed his hand and he could sense her worry as well. And her excitement.

He could almost feel her monitoring the engines as he was, beside him completely in all areas of the ship.

The engines were powering up, slowly at first, then as they stabilized after such a long voyage, their power increased.

"Full power and stable," Fisher said.

Roscoe had known that a moment before Fisher spoke.

Around the room everyone cheered.

"At full power," Roscoe said, "how long until we reach full stop?"

"Seven months and three days," Hudson said from his station.

The cheering stopped as the situation that both Roscoe and Maria knew already sank in.

"*Morning Song,*" Maria asked. "May Chairman Mundy and I leave the chairs and possibly the ship and still be in contact with you?"

Yes.

Roscoe instantly knew that in the arm of his chair and Maria's chair was a small needle that would implant a device to allow them to keep in contact with the *Morning Song.*

"Please insert the device," Roscoe said.

"Yes, please," Maria said.

Roscoe felt a slight sting.

"Everyone please do a full check of the systems attached to your panels," Maria said.

Roscoe and Maria both did the same, going over every detail of the ship to make sure that *Morning Song* was stable and slowing.

Then Roscoe took the final precaution. "*Morning Song,* is the ship stable and slowing?"

Yes.

"Do you see any signs of weakness in any system or engine?" Roscoe asked.

No, but repairs need to be made after full stop.

"We understand that," Maria said. "And they will be done. Thank you."

"We are planning on taking a break now and working toward getting more help on board," Roscoe said. "Do you see any problem with that?"

No, but please return to the command chairs as soon as possible to continue your training and education.

"We will," Maria said.

With that, Roscoe stood and pulled Maria gently to her feet. He could still feel he was connected, melded in a way with her in so many ways, ways he didn't yet fully understand.

She stood, still holding his hand.

He could sense her reluctance to let go. Her beautiful golden eyes were almost swirling with all the new information.

Around them the big Command Center was silent as everyone watched them.

Finally, he nodded to her. And together they let go of each other's hand.

He could still sense her, still felt meshed with her, and could still feel all the systems in the big ship around them.

She looked around, then smiled at him. "Seems you're stuck with me for a while."

"For a lot longer than a while, I hope," he said.

At that, everyone in the big Command Center broke into cheers and applause and together, they turned to the crew and took a bow.

CHAPTER 27

"We're going to need to talk to Chairman Ray," Maria said after the cheering died down.

"He and everyone on his ship have been watching," Callie said, smiling. "As best they can with the time deletion. We've been moving in real fast motion as far as they are concerned."

Roscoe laughed at the idea of that.

Maria really didn't want to just talk with Ray out in the open. And she could sense that Roscoe did not either.

"*Morning Song*," Maria said into the air. "Can we personally transport away from the ship and return?"

On the wall-sized monitor in front of the room the word "Yes" appeared.

"Will we still be in contact with you and the systems of the ship?"

Again the word "Yes" appeared.

"Thank you, *Morning Song*," Maria said.

Maria knew from everything she had learned that normal procedure for a *Morning Song* crew was to leave at least five in the Command Center at all times. A pilot, a person at security, and three engineers.

Roscoe knew that as well and turned to his second-in-command,

Jonas, who had been assigned the security main post. "Stay at your post until I return."

Jonas nodded.

Maria looked at Hudson. "Please stay at your station."

Hudson nodded, his eyes wide from all he had learned in the quick training. He was so eager to learn all the time and all this sudden knowledge must really be messing with his balance.

"Callie, you have command while we are gone," Roscoe said. "But please avoid those chairs."

She laughed and pointed down at her station in front of her. "Right here is just fine."

They picked two other engineers to stay as well, then Roscoe told the rest of them to jump back to Fisher and Callie's ship and get something to eat and rest. Until they got help, all of them would be doing long shifts.

Then Maria turned to Fisher. "You are with us."

He nodded.

She then turned to Roscoe. "Do the honors, partner."

He smiled, took her hand, and jumped all three of them to the bridge of Chairman Ray's ship.

Chairman Ray was sitting in his command chair, watching the big screen in front of him that showed the Command Center of the *Morning Song.*

As they appeared, he and Tacita both jumped to their feet. Then they both did something that Maria would have never imagined them doing in her entire long life.

He and Tacita both bowed to her and Roscoe.

And everyone else on the bridge bowed to them as well.

"Welcome, Chairmen," Chairman Ray said.

She looked at Roscoe who clearly was as shocked as she felt. She could sense his shock and how really deep it ran. Somehow, Roscoe managed to speak. She wasn't sure how. She would not have been able to.

"Can we talk in a private area?" Roscoe asked.

An instant later the five of them were in a large meeting room. It was filled with a long conference table with a white top with a dozen cloth office chairs around it. A large screen, now blank, filled one wall.

The lighting was indirect and bright and there was no smell at all.

A completely sterile-looking room and Maria wondered why anyone would have a room like this one.

Chairman Ray and Tacita took the chairs near one end on the far side of the table, Fisher took the chair in front of him across from Ray and Tacita, clearly just as puzzled as she and Roscoe were.

She and Roscoe took the chairs at the end of the big table.

"So what was all that about?" Roscoe asked.

Maria let her knee move against his leg and could feel his strength and energy just from the touch.

"You both have been chosen for a very honored position among Seeders," Ray said. He looked at Tacita and she nodded.

So Chairman Ray looked back at them and leaned forward. "This was why you were picked for this mission. We hoped that if we figured out a way to get inside, *Morning Song* would accept you both."

Maria sat back and just stared at Ray.

They had known about Seeder Mother Ships. She couldn't believe that. Why hadn't they said something?

"They have not had time for the history of the Seeders," Tacita said, touching her husband's arm gently. "They do not understand, but they will. They have much to learn, as I am sure *Morning Song* told them."

Ray nodded. "You are right, we have a more pressing problem to deal with first."

Maria just sat there, staring at Ray.

Again it was Roscoe who seemed to find his footing a little faster than she did. "We need to save millions."

Now it was Ray's turn to look puzzled. Then he laughed. "You already did that."

Roscoe looked at Fisher, then at Maria.

Maria sat forward. "And just how did we do that?"

"By taking control of the ship, stopping the malfunction, turning the ship around, and starting to brake," Ray said.

Suddenly Maria understood. "We are not letting the ship jump to one-hundred-light-year trans-tunnel flights."

It took a moment, but Roscoe started to laugh and then Fisher followed.

"It's going to take a few hundred years or more at this sub-light speed," Ray said, "for that ship to even reach the edge of the Milky Way, even without braking."

"Oh, thank the heavens," Maria said, leaning back and staring at the ceiling. She couldn't believe how completely relieved she felt. And she could sense Roscoe beside her feeling relieved and happy as well.

They had accomplished their mission.

"So what's the pressing problem we need to face now?"

Ray started to speak, but Tacita touched his arm and shook her head.

Then Tacita sat forward and looked directly at Maria with a dark intensity that Maria had never seen before.

"You need to go back to *Morning Song* and continue your education. Then we can talk."

"Can we at least get help manning the big ship?"

"In four weeks," Ray said, "your speed will be slow enough for us to match with our normal ships and start sending crew aboard. And you will need to pick most of them and a command crew. Until then, I'm afraid it's just the fifteen of you. You will do fine. *Morning Song* is a very good ship."

Then Ray and Tacita stood and bowed slightly to her and Roscoe.

"Please excuse us," Ray said. "Time is short and we have a lot to do."

With that, they both vanished, leaving Fisher, Roscoe, and Maria half out of their chairs.

Maria had no idea at all what just happened.

None.

CHAPTER 28

Roscoe jumped them back on board *Morning Song* and into Fisher's ship inside the big scanning room. He instantly felt better.

"That's amazing," Maria said. "I feel like I'm home."

"I think we are," Roscoe said, smiling at her.

"So either of you have any idea what just happened?" Fisher asked. "If you do, you can explain it to me as I get us something to eat."

They followed Fisher into the kitchen and Roscoe sat down at the dining table and Maria sat beside him, her hand resting on his leg, keeping the connection between them. That connection seemed to be growing stronger by the moment and Roscoe liked that more than he wanted to admit.

He wanted her to be a part of him. And he had a hunch that if she wasn't close, he would no longer feel whole.

Just as being away from *Morning Song* didn't feel right.

"I think that Ray and Tacita knew right from the start what the big ship was," Maria said.

"I agree," Roscoe said. "But I have no idea why they didn't tell us."

"And how do they know?" Maria asked. "My sense is that they have sat in a joint command chair at some point in the past."

125

"Could they really be that old?" Fisher asked as he pulled out bread and some cut turkey to make sandwiches with.

"Nothing stopping any of us from getting very, very old," Maria said. "*Morning Song* promised us history and far more education. Seems we need that."

"I agree completely," Roscoe said. "Maybe after that we will understand why they didn't tell us what this ship was in the first place. And what they were in such a hurry to go do."

Then he sat back enjoying the feel of Maria beside him as they planned crew rotation onto the *Morning Song* Command Center.

About halfway through the quick lunch, Roscoe suddenly had a thought. "You can't count Maria and me as part of that rotation."

She looked at him and then nodded, clearly understanding.

"We're going to be in school," Roscoe said.

"And at times we might not actually be on board," Maria said.

"That's possible as well," he said, nodding. "It's up to you to just keep this big ship braking and stable while we learn what we can about what we are up against and what comes next."

Fisher just shook his head and said, "I'll do my best."

Roscoe smiled at Fisher. "She's a good ship. She'll help you."

"I hope so," Fisher said.

After they finished, Roscoe took Maria's hand, enjoying the feel and the energy running through it to him.

"Ready to go to class?"

"As I'll ever be," she said, smiling at him and then quickly kissing him.

This kiss surprised them both because even more energy flowed between them and a lot more caring and feeling.

It was so passionate in just a slight kiss, it took his breath away.

"Well, that's going to be interesting," she said, touching her lips and then smiling at him.

She was flushed and breathing hard.

"And that's an understatement," he said.

"What just happened there?" Fisher asked, frowning at them.

Maria laughed. "More information than you want to know."

Fisher blushed and turned away to clean up the dishes. "Meet you in the Command Center."

Roscoe and Maria both laughed, then holding hands, jumped back to the heart and soul and brains of *Morning Song*.

CHAPTER 29

M aria stood in front of the two command chairs, holding hands with Roscoe. A tiny part of her was worried about sitting down again, but honestly, she felt excited about the learning she knew was coming.

"How did it go with Chairman Ray?" Callie asked.

"Interesting describes it," Roscoe said. "Fisher will explain. He'll be here in a moment."

She nodded.

Maria pulled Roscoe toward the two chairs. "We have some lessons to learn."

"Looking forward to it," he said, squeezing her hand.

Then they turned and sat down, scooting back into the form-fitting chairs and making sure they had a solid hold of each other's hands.

Again the blue heads-up screen came up in front of them and Maria could again feel her mind expanding even more.

She and Roscoe both did a quick check of all the ship's major systems.

"Everything seems to functioning fine," Maria said.

"Better than can be expected after such a long trip," Roscoe said. "*Morning Song*, you have done a great job over the long voyage."

Words appeared on the translucent blue screen in front of them.

. . .

Thank you, Chairmen.

Are you ready for the next stage?

"We are," Maria said.

The form of the chairs shifted and encased them quickly in a tight but comfortable shell. She still held Roscoe's hand, but could see nothing at all.

There was no sense of movement at all, but within just a few seconds the big chairs opened back up.

They were now sitting in a large circular room, their two chairs on a higher level looking out over what looked like a comfortable living room. Five steps led down into the round center of the room.

Long couches, large overstuffed chairs, coffee tables, all formed in groups in the large room like a lounge, or a very comfortable waiting area. The floor seemed to have a carpet of some sort on it and everything was in brown tones.

Maria guessed that the room might hold a hundred people without trouble, and there were enough couches and chairs for more than that. It was an immense round room. But at the same time it had numbers of areas where just a few people could talk and feel private.

The ceiling was far overhead and the light indirect. The only thing she could smell was a faint scent of bread cooking.

Maria knew that they were supposed to stand and just make themselves at home. So they both did stand, looking around, but keeping their hands together.

Maria was amazed. The huge room, even for its size, felt very, very comfortable.

Maria had a sense where they were, but she didn't want to think about that being possible.

Roscoe pointed at the wide area where their two chairs sat. "Landing areas for a good fifty sets of chairs around the room. See the marks on the floor?"

She did and she agreed. This is where the Chairmen came.

At that moment another set of command chairs shimmered into existence about a quarter turn around the circle away from them.

Maria remained holding Roscoe's hand as the new command chairs opened and Chairman Ray and Tacita stood, smiling.

Of all the people she had expected to see here for their training, it was not them. Not after the way they had acted on their ship just a short time ago.

Chairman Ray, his long gray hair flowing behind him, stepped down into the main part of the room with Tacita at his side.

Roscoe glanced at her, then led them down the five steps.

"Where are we?" Maria asked as they got near Chairman Ray.

"Earth," Ray said, smiling.

"All human cultures name their home world Earth," Roscoe said, annoyed at the dance of an answer.

But Maria knew what Ray meant. She had to just let him say it.

"The first Earth," Ray said, still smiling and indicating they should sit on a comfortable-looking couch. "This is the home world of all the Seeders."

Maria just couldn't breathe.

It felt like something heavy was on her chest.

It wasn't possible.

She knew that the Seeder home world was just a myth. She never expected to be here.

Yet she knew, with her connection to *Morning Song*, that Ray was telling the truth.

She was on Earth.

Not her Earth or Roscoe's Earth.

The first Earth.

CHAPTER 30

Roscoe could sense how upset Maria was and squeezed her hand some and guided her to sit down beside him on one of the soft-looking couches.

As they sat, the couch shifted slightly and molded perfectly to their forms.

Ray and Tacita sat across from them, both smiling.

"We are sorry about our deception on my ship," Ray said. "We knew you were going to go back to the *Morning Song* and immediately jump here for your training and we needed to get to our ship to get here as well to greet you and help you get started and answer questions we couldn't answer with Chairman Fisher present."

"Where is your Mother Ship located?" Maria asked.

"In the spiral galaxy that is named The Sevens by the residents there," Tacita said, her voice soft for the first time that Maria had ever heard. "It's the same spiral galaxy that *Morning Song* originated from."

"It is our base," Ray said. "Our ship is called *Warm Night*. We built the *Morning Song* there along with her sister ship, *Morning Breeze*, who is coming into the Milky Way in about forty thousand years on the same path."

"You built them?" Maria asked, trying to wrap her head around how old the two sitting across from them really were.

"We did," Tacita said, nodding.

"Maria and I are the first Chairmen of the *Morning Song*?" Roscoe asked, clearly as surprised as Maria felt.

"The only ones there will ever be unless there is an accident or you have a desire to step down," Ray said. "She is your ship and your companion from the moment you sat down and she accepted you."

Maria had nothing to say.

Neither did Roscoe it seemed.

Ray smiled. "I assume since you had just gotten here you have eaten before coming?"

"We did," Maria managed to say.

"Good," Ray said, standing. "We will jump back when your first training is complete to help in answering any questions you might have."

"Just stay seated," Tacita said as she stood beside Ray.

Then they turned and moved toward their command chairs.

And at that moment a simple bubble surrounded Maria and Roscoe and collapsed in skin-tight on them.

Maria only had a moment to even think about it before the images came flooding in.

And for the first time, she started to really understand that even though she had been an expert, how little she had known about Seeders.

And their history.

CHAPTER 31

As the bubble that had wrapped around them dropped and Roscoe let the last of the images fade away, he shook his head. It felt like he had had so much information crammed into his mind, it would be impossible to remember it all.

But somehow, it felt like he did.

Around them the large circular room hadn't changed at all.

He was still holding Maria's hand and he turned to face her.

"You all right?"

"I think so," she said, blinking her wonderful golden eyes. He could feel so much more of their attraction now and all he wanted to do was hold her in his arms.

She moved over and leaned into him and he put his arm around her.

"This feels perfect."

"It does," he said.

They sat there silently like that for a good minute, just not talking. Roscoe was lost in all the information he had been given, and in his incredible feeling for Maria.

Two command chairs shimmered into place and again Chairman Ray and Tacita got out and came toward them.

"How long were we in that information flow?" Roscoe asked, describing what had happened to them in the best way he could.

"Three hours," Ray said.

"Food will be brought in for all of us," Tacita said, "and we can answer questions as you have them."

"I'm not sure what I know and don't know," Maria said.

"That feeling will pass with time as your mind organizes everything," Ray said.

Roscoe nodded.

"Can you help me," Maria said, "if possible, understand a timeline structure for the Seeders."

"Of course," Ray said. "It was your passion before this, I would have assumed it would remain your passion."

Roscoe was just going to let her lead on this. He needed the same thing, a way to organize the vast amount of information that had flowed into his mind in the last few hours.

"The Seeders originated on this planet?" she asked. "The first Earth as it is called."

"Yes," Ray said.

"And as they managed to make it into space and discovered trans-tunnel drive, they spread out and discovered they were alone in the universe."

"They were alone in this galaxy, yes," Ray said.

Roscoe was following all of this and having Maria talk it out loud really was helping him organize his mind as well.

"And as they spread out, they developed the techniques the frontline Seeders use now in terraforming appropriate planets," Maria said, "and then seeding them with human life and plant life from their original home world."

"Yes," Ray said. "But in those first few hundred thousand years in this galaxy, they learned the hard lesson about the falseness of non-intervention in growing human civilizations. It was not a smooth road to galaxy-wide stability."

Roscoe nodded, remembering all that very clearly now as Ray put it in clear form.

"After this galaxy stabilized," Ray said, "and became very advanced, faster ships were built from a series of really lucky inventions and we were able to jump to a nearby galaxy. We again found no other intelligent life."

"So they seeded it," Maria said, nodding.

"Yes," Ray said. "And continued on until in one galaxy the explorers ran across alien life, a young civilization they called The Ants because of their heritage."

Roscoe could see The Ants clearly in his mind. Very close to Earth ants, only the size of small dogs and with advanced hive minds. When humans had discovered them, The Ants had managed to get into space, but only barely.

"We left that galaxy alone and moved around them," Ray said, "not bothering them."

"They are now extinct?" Maria said simply.

"Sadly, yes," Ray said. "But we have not touched their galaxy in any fashion in case some of their members have survived."

"Seven alien races, seven galaxies skipped," Roscoe said, clearly getting the images of each alien race. None of them felt threatening in any fashion in his teaching. And four of the seven were now extinct. None of the four had yet to make it out of their own home system.

Roscoe knew there was an entire branch of Seeders who did nothing but study and look for new life forms. They always moved ahead of any Seeder frontline into a galaxy to make sure there were no aliens in that galaxy anywhere.

"That is correct," Ray said, answering Roscoe's statement about how humans skip entire galaxies with hints of alien races.

Tacita finally added to the discussion. "To answer the next question, no one really knows exactly how many galaxies humans have spread over. The galaxy this original planet is in cannot be seen from the Milky Way."

"That far?" Roscoe asked, again not being able to comprehend the distance.

"That far. No number really describes the distance," Ray said.

"How many Mother Seeder ships are there?" Maria asked.

Roscoe was surprised he didn't have that information in the giant information load they had taken in.

"At the moment there are twenty-eight of us," Ray said. "Counting your ship. Fourteen more ships are in transit as the *Morning Song* did, but we hope without the programmed braking problem. Ten more are under construction in various galaxies."

"We need many, many more," Tacita said.

Ray only nodded to that.

"And our mission," Roscoe said, "is to crew and stock the *Morning Song* and head out from the Milky Way in a new direction?"

"That is the basics of it," Ray said.

Maria squeezed Roscoe's hand to signal there was more that Ray wasn't saying, but Roscoe had caught that as well.

"But you want us to go in a certain direction," Roscoe said, "that has some possible problems, correct?"

Ray and Tacita both sat there staring at them, then Ray nodded slowly. "Yes. We have heard that there may be another galaxy-spanning race in the direction we would like you and *Morning Song* to go."

Suddenly he and Maria being picked for this made sense.

He looked at Ray and nodded. "You picked Military and History and a lot of brains to lead this because you think we may need both in what we run into. And we are from a young galaxy still able to think without centuries of training into Seeder dogma."

Ray and Tacita nodded.

"After a time of growth and steady worlds, humans by nature are very pacifistic," Ray said. "We would stand little to no chance against an aggressive alien race who didn't like us. We don't even like large governments and when not needed, we disband them."

"Did you know this alien race might be out there," Maria asked, "when you sent the leading edge of Seeders and the *Morning Song* over a million years ago toward the Milky Way?"

"Yes," Ray said bluntly. "We need you to recruit fighters as well as workers and arm *Morning Song* for a fight if needed."

"The empty hanger," Roscoe said. "A fighter deck."

"Yes," Ray said. "And when the second ship arrives in forty thousand years, it will recruit from Andromeda and head out in a similar, but slightly different direction to see what it can find."

"And you have not scouted this alien race in any fashion?" Roscoe asked.

"We have some," Ray said. "From what we can tell, their main galaxy a million years ago was about thirty galaxies from the Milky Way, but we have no idea if they are now advancing or not in any direction. We really know little about them. All of this will be in the final educational session in ten days. One thing at a time."

Roscoe didn't much like waiting on something as important as that, but he understood. And Maria's hand in his helped him.

At that moment a table appeared between them, their seats on the couch lifted them to a comfortable dining position close to the table, and then food appeared.

Turkey, gravy, rolls, and more potatoes and dressing than any four people could eat in a week.

And it smelled heavenly. Until that moment Roscoe didn't realize just how hungry he had become.

"Eat," Ray said. "Then return to *Morning Song* and rest. Tomorrow will be another long day of learning."

"Can our minds handle this kind of information flow for ten more days?" Roscoe asked.

Ray and Tacita both smiled. Then Tacita said simply. "Yes, and you have only begun the learning. It will continue for life."

Then she leaned forward and grabbed a large drumstick as Roscoe just sat there until Maria pushed him to start eating.

SECTION THREE:

AN UNDERSTANDING OF POWER

CHAPTER 32

When Maria and Roscoe returned to *Morning Song*, both Callie and Fisher came running down to the lower level of the Command Center to face them. They were both clearly very happy and relieved.

Behind them the big screen showed the open space and in the distance was the Milky Way Galaxy, filling a quarter of the screen with its billions of suns.

Maria felt like she was once again home and could feel herself relax.

She and Roscoe both did a quick scan of *Morning Song* to make sure she was doing all right. Everything seemed perfectly in balance and the big ship was still braking. After they got down far enough to allow other crew to come on board, they could start some of the major repairs that were needed.

Maria smiled at Callie and Fisher as she and Roscoe stood, continuing to hold hands. "We didn't know we were leaving like that or we would have warned you."

"Yeah, a surprise," Roscoe said.

"Where did you go?" Fisher asked.

"A long ways away to do a training session in the history of Seeders," Maria said.

"Every day we will be doing another," Roscoe said, "I suppose on different topics, so this will be normal. Are you all right here?"

"We are," Fisher nodded. "We're doing eight hour shifts and rotating."

"Great," Maria said.

Roscoe looked at her and smiled. "You up for a little exploring before we get some rest and go back to class?

"I'd love that," she said, smiling, a surge of excitement running through her. Even though she knew the seeder history now and she really understood this ship, she wanted to see it all for herself.

Roscoe looked at Fisher. "Call if you need our help. And *Morning Song*, please help them and keep us informed."

On the image of space that filled the large front screen, the letters formed.

I will.

"Thank you, *Morning Song*," Maria said.

Then Roscoe squeezed her hand and jumped them.

As they arrived, the lights came up.

They were standing in a huge, multi-leveled room with a giant fireplace in the center far wall. It did not have furniture, but Maria could imagine this big room with art, furniture, and a crackling fire in the fireplace being amazingly comfortable.

It felt comfortable and like a home even without furniture.

The floor had a soft substance that felt like carpet on it, but she knew from her knowledge of the ship that it wasn't. It was part of the decking and could be altered to be as thick or as hard or any color that anyone wanted.

She knew exactly where they were. Roscoe had jumped them to the Chairmen's Suite.

Their suite.

"Wow," she said, looking around.

Hand-in-hand, they moved to look at the huge master bedroom and bath with a giant shower and a wonderful-looking tub that she knew she could spend hours in soaking and reading.

They both knew that the water systems in the big ship would need some major work to be up to full function after the long voyage. *Morning Song* had robots working on it, but they were making very little progress. So neither of them suggested using the big shower.

Each of them had their own office in the large suite attached as well, each office with its own bathroom attached.

There was also a huge kitchen and nice sized dining area that could hold a table for ten easily. And there was a larger dining area that could hold thirty people.

Even totally empty, this space felt wonderful and she knew, without a doubt, she could be home and very comfortable living here.

She turned and kissed Roscoe.

As with the kiss in the kitchen, the simple kiss took on entirely new levels of passion and intensity.

It felt like she was making love to him at that moment.

Through the kiss she felt even closer to him and more blended with him and clearly in love with this stunning man.

She pressed herself against him and he pushed back, standing there in the doorway of their future kitchen, kissing.

Kissing and so much more.

More passion than she had ever felt in her life.

Finally, he broke the kiss and stood there breathing hard as if he had run a fast mile.

She felt the same way. She felt like a schoolgirl getting a first kiss, excited and breathless, yet at the same time she felt like she had just made love to Roscoe for thirty minutes.

"Wow," was all she said.

He smiled and nodded to that, still breathing hard, his dark eyes staring into hers.

Finally, he turned and indicated the big suite with a sweep of his arm. "You like the place?"

"Do you?" she asked, holding his hand and pushing her shoulder into his arm.

"I do if you'll live here with me," he said, turning to face her again.

"Are you asking me to move in with you?" she asked, smiling at him. "We've only known each other less than a month."

"I am," he said, smiling right back.

"Then I love the place if I am living here with you."

She kissed him again, and once again it felt as if they were making love just standing there, pressed against each other, kissing.

When she broke the kiss that time, she laughed.

He was again breathing hard.

Then for the first time in hours, she let go of his hand and walked down the few steps to the area in front of the big fireplace, slowly taking her clothes off as she went.

Behind her she heard Roscoe say, "*Morning Song*, please do not allow scans of this suite."

In her mind she knew that *Morning Song* had agreed.

"Thank you, *Morning Song*," she said as she kicked her pants aside and turned to face the man she planned on spending a long time with.

He had his shirt off and he was staring at her naked body in a way that only a man could stare.

And she loved it.

She lay down on the fairly soft carpet-like flooring and smiled up at him as he struggled to get his pants off.

Then finally, he was on top of her and inside her.

And the passion was so great, she came almost instantly as the two of them melded both minds and bodies.

CHAPTER 33

For the next ten days, Roscoe and Maria went back to the big education and meeting room. Within minutes each time, Ray and Tacita joined them to prep them for the day's learning and answer questions and eat dinner with them when it was finished.

Roscoe felt like his mind was going to explode each day when the session was finished. One day was completely on the process of terraforming a planet. Another was on trans-tunnel mechanics, another was about political and governmental systems, the patterns humans took in growing cultures, and how to stop wars.

Ten topics total until the final day.

And every day he and Maria had gone back to *Morning Song* to check on the status of their ship, to help the tiring crew where they could, to make love, and then sleep.

They had used a few hours each day to explore their ship, including spending one hour just walking between the huge Seeder ships secured to one of the two major flight decks.

Even in an hour, they didn't get very far. There were so many ships and they were all so large. Even understanding it, the size and scope stunned Roscoe.

Finally they went back for their tenth lesson. Today it was about the coming mission.

This lesson worried Roscoe and Maria more than anything. They knew their mission on *Morning Song* was to seed new galaxies with human life, but they also knew they had to determine who the other major race was and that race's intentions.

So before they went under the bubble in the big room, Chairman Ray said, "We'll stay until you are finished this time."

And when they were finished, Roscoe finally understood why Chairman Ray had stayed. The aliens were very real and very powerful.

But they weren't aliens. They were humans.

It seems in the first education day, they had left out a pretty important galaxy-wide war that had happened in the first galaxy.

An off-shoot human culture from this galaxy called Lotus, after their first great, warlike leader, were the threats close to the Milky Way.

"That is not what I expected," Roscoe said after the bubble dropped and they could talk.

Maria squeezed his hand. He could tell she was as upset as he was. He would have rather been fighting alien spiders or intelligent raccoons or something.

Chairman Ray and Tacita were sitting across from them, worried looks on both of their faces.

"Now you understand why we could not scout them very well," Ray said.

"We could not allow them to know we were even close in any fashion," Tacita said, "you were given all the information we have about them and their culture."

Roscoe nodded. "Trans-tunnel flight, a desire to expand, they do not do terraforming, but instead leave planets the way they were and just take over and make bases and control the life there in a war-like way."

"Yes, when this galaxy's sane cultures finally cornered them and defeated them, we banned the survivors from this part of the universe," Ray said.

Roscoe nodded, the teaching clear in his head and starting to make sense.

"You built what was effectively the first Seeder Mother Ship called *Dark Night*," Roscoe said, "put the remaining four million members all in suspended animation, and sent the ship at full trans-tunnel continuous drive for six hundred thousand years."

"Yes," Ray said. "To a galaxy so far away, it never occurred to anyone at the time we would get close to it millions of years later."

"And you made sure *Dark Night* would never fly at top speeds again once it reached that galaxy," Maria said, nodding. "Thus trapping them in the one galaxy unless they made huge scientific jumps."

"Yes," Ray said. "And honestly, after so much time, we had basically forgotten about them until scout ships searching for alien life ahead of seeding realized how close they were to the target galaxy and pulled back."

Roscoe tried accessing a question he had and couldn't find it, so he asked. "You have no evidence that they have left their one galaxy?"

"That is correct," Ray said. "It is a hope we all share that they have not. The scout ships that realized where it was at in relation to the target galaxy came back into known space to report."

"But two million years ago they still survived in that galaxy," Ray said. "We will need you and your scouts from *Morning Song* to determine if they have expanded, very carefully."

"So we will not get near or seed any of the closest galaxies to theirs," Maria said.

"Again, a plan we think wise," Ray said.

Roscoe nodded to Maria. "We can deal with this."

"Can you see why we wanted new Chairmen with your abilities and youth?" Ray asked.

"We will need to maintain a military posture on *Morning Song*," Roscoe said, understanding completely. As Ray had said, advanced human cultures become pacifists and forget how to fight eventually.

"And I am needed to use my skills and talents," Maria said, "to map this area of the known universe in a way that makes sense and make sure all Seeders close are aware of restricted territories."

"Yes," Tacita said.

"But I have a question," Maria said. "Why do the Seeders have no historical memory past what we have been trained here? Why are entire galaxies of humans just left on their own to let the knowledge of Seeders drop into myth or religion?"

"Human nature," Tacita said. "When there is no threat to home or life, humans don't care about the past or what's even on the other side of their own planet."

"For a few hundred galaxies," Rays said, "when we first left this galaxy, we tried to maintain a cultural memory with those we helped start. But it never held and no one seemed to care."

Roscoe had seen that already at a much smaller scale, more than he wanted to admit. It was already happening in the Milky Way and Seeders were still everywhere in every culture there, helping them along.

"Well," Maria said firmly, "with the Lotus as neighbors, forgetting is not an option. So for the Local Group of galaxies and the ones we seed, we will change that practice."

Ray and Tacita both nodded, then smiled.

"They are smiling," Roscoe said to Maria, "because they are proud they picked us."

"We are proud," Ray said, laughing.

At that, the dinner table rose from the ground again and food appeared, steaming and smelling wonderful.

As they turned to dig into the roast beef and steamed vegetables, Roscoe decided he had one more question that he had been wondering about every day since he saw this big place.

"Do all the Chairmen meet at any point?"

"Once a year on the anniversary of the launching of the first Seeder Mother Ship," Ray said.

"And when is that?" Maria said. "How many standard days away?"

"Two-hundred-and-six days," Tacita said.

"How long ago did it launch?" Roscoe asked, wondering why all this information wasn't in the information flow in their minds.

"Just over six million years ago," Tacita said.

"Whose ship was that?" Maria asked as she dug into a pile of mashed potatoes that looked heavenly.

"Ours," Ray said, smiling as he took a second slice of roast beef with one hand and reached out and touched Tacita's shoulder fondly with the other.

Roscoe had a first bite of roast beef almost to his mouth when Ray said that.

Eventually, the bite made it all the way.

Eventually.

CHAPTER 34

Over the next ten days as they got *Morning Song* slowed enough to start taking on crew, Maria and Roscoe jumped to many various ships to start the hiring of crew.

Mother Ships worked just as any other Seeder ship. It was basically a corporation that hired crew and paid them. Any crew member could leave at any point and settle on a planet.

Living on the ship was cheap, far less than any salary working on a Seeder ship, so all crew members saved most of their income and often retired to a favorite planet after only a decade or so. Some were lifers, not caring much about the money, using it to help others where they could.

Maria had talked with Roscoe at different times about how he felt about spending such a long time with her, especially after they learned how really old Ray and Tacita were. The answer that Roscoe gave that finally satisfied her was "I'll tell you in a few thousand years."

She had really liked the sound of that and had kissed him and they almost hadn't gotten back to work.

But they had because of the amount of work they had to do.

They were faced with what seemed like an impossible task. They had an empty ship that was in need of some pretty extensive repairs after its million-plus years in space.

The warehouses were stocked with furniture, parts, and just about anything else needed on board the ship except for food. So bringing in food and getting the kitchens up and running would be fairly high on the list.

And the water system was a mess and had to be upgraded completely after so many years of lack of use. In fact, the ship had never been used, so many of the problems were new-built problems, even though the ship was so old.

Repairing water systems and major support systems was top on the list and could be done as the ship continued to slow, as soon as they got help on board.

Maria had come to love the ship, though, over the twenty days. She could feel *Morning Song* with her at every moment and loved that. She talked to *Morning Song* a lot and where possible, *Morning Song* would answer on a nearby screen.

But as the twenty days went on, she had also just fallen more and more in love with Roscoe. She felt she was blended with him, yet they were both very distinct people.

They often finished each other's sentences and they laughed a lot.

And they made love every day. With each lovemaking session, she felt even closer to him.

Making love, they became one person.

And one of them was always touching the other it seemed. They gained energy from contact.

On the day they decided to let the first ship try to dock with the *Morning Song*, she and Roscoe were in their command chairs. They had decided that Roscoe's former ship, *The Huntington*, should try first. It was the fastest of all the Seeder ships at sub-light speeds.

On the bridge beside them at one station was Fisher on Roscoe's right and on the other side Callie on Maria's left. The two of them just felt comfortable now in those third and fourth command positions. Maria liked them there.

All fifteen on board *Morning Song* were in the Command Center, leaving Fisher and Callie's ship, *The Lady*, empty.

"First, *Morning Song*," Maria said, studying her heads-up display, "we need to move *The Lady* to one side of the big landing bay."

On the big screen in front of them was the image of *The Lady* sitting in the middle of the huge landing bay.

"A position close to Entrance 63," Roscoe said.

Maria knew that was the entrance they had used on their jumps to the Command Center the first time.

"Can we do that?"

The word "Yes" appeared in the middle of the big screen.

"Everyone, monitor your stations," Roscoe said.

"Go ahead, *Morning Song*," Maria said.

The Lady vanished from its position on the big dock and appeared near one wall, still looking very small.

Maria could tell that all systems were stable.

"Very good, *Morning Song*," Maria said.

The words *Thank you* appeared on the big screen over the image of the mostly empty landing dock.

"Power down engines to full shut-down," Roscoe said.

Maria watched the systems closely as the engines slowly powered down. They had decided it would be easier for a ship to match a constant speed than one that was changing every second.

"Engines powering down," Fisher reported, more for the rest of the crew, since she and Roscoe got the information slightly ahead of everyone through their big chairs.

"Atmosphere shield on the docking bay door seems to be functioning," Hudson said from a station behind her.

"Engines shut down," Fisher reported. "Everything stable."

Maria shifted the image on the big screen to show *The Huntington* matching speeds with them just outside the big bay door.

Red, who was now Chairman of *The Huntington*, came over the link. "Speeds matched. Engines off."

"Open the bay doors," Maria said.

The bay doors seemed to hesitate for a moment, then slid back in four directions.

Maria knew they would need to be serviced as well, but for the moment they were working.

"Atmosphere shield holding," Hudson said.

"*Morning Song*," Maria said. "Please bring *The Huntington* on board."

155

Maria knew a tractor beam had taken a firm grip around *The Huntington* and was pulling it in through the doors.

"Wow, some perspective," Roscoe said.

Maria was stunned as well. "*The Huntington* was the biggest warship the Seeders had built in Andromeda, and yet coming in through the big bay doors, it looked almost like a toy hanging there.

"Middle of the deck is fine, *Morning Song*," Roscoe said. "They won't be staying that long."

The Huntington drifted over the massive deck and eased to the surface.

"Closing bay doors," Maria said.

"Tractor beam released," Roscoe said.

A moment later Red and Mattie's faces came across clear on the big screen. "Welcome to the *Morning Song*," Roscoe said, smiling at his old friends from Sector Justice.

"Wow," was all Red could say.

"Bring engines back to full. Let's keep slowing down," Roscoe said.

"Engines coming back up slowly," Fisher said.

Maria and Roscoe both stayed in the big chair until the engines were up and running smoothly and the ship was stable.

"Thank you, *Morning Song*," Maria said, standing and pulling Roscoe up as well.

"Very well done," Roscoe said.

The words *Thank you* again appeared on the big screen.

"Hudson, you have Command Center," Roscoe said. "Everyone stay to rotations for now. Help has arrived.

Hudson's head snapped up and his eyes were wide.

Maria squeezed Roscoe's hand for being so mean, and barely stopped a laugh at Hudson's look. He would be fine, just as Roscoe knew he would. Plus, *Morning Song* would warn them if something was going wrong.

Roscoe turned to Fisher and Callie. "Want to meet our first guests?"

"Love to," Callie said.

And a moment later Roscoe had the four of them in the Command Center of *The Huntington*.

156

And after the first twenty minutes of explaining the size and scope of *Morning Song*, Maria realized that they had one more important task that needed to be done very quickly. There needed to be an introduction video to *Morning Song* that everyone was required to watch.

Before coming on board.

CHAPTER 35

t took another twenty days for the crew of *The Huntington* to take over some of Command Center duties and start repairs.

The fifteen original members on Fisher's ship remained there, sleeping and eating together, since they had all become friends. Roscoe liked those dinners since Fisher was such a great cook.

He and Maria had borrowed an extra bed and transported it to their suite on *Morning Song* because they just didn't want to keep everyone awake with their lovemaking. Besides, even without furniture, they loved their suite.

The crew of *The Huntington* bunked and ate on board ship, since repairs to the water systems on *Morning Song* were far from started, let alone completed.

Roscoe and Maria had been talking and wanted to offer the second-in-command to Fisher and Callie. But they weren't sure how to go about it. So one afternoon as things were calm, they jumped to Chairman Ray and Tacita's ship after asking the day before if they could.

They ended up back in the sterile meeting room and both Ray and Tacita were happy to see them.

"How is the learning settling in?" Ray asked as they all took seats,

Ray and Tacita on one side, Roscoe and Maria on the other. As they always did, Roscoe and Maria moved so their legs would be in contact.

Roscoe shrugged. "I know the knowledge is there and I find myself knowing something suddenly when I need to know it, but I have no memory of knowing the information before. I'm no longer surprised at that happening."

Maria laughed. "Describes my experience exactly."

"It will get smoother with time," Tacita said.

Roscoe glanced at Maria and she nodded that he should go ahead. "We are wondering if we can offer the job of second-in-command of the upcoming mission to Fisher and Callie."

Ray sat back, smiling.

Tacita shook her head. "You can offer any job on the *Morning Song* to anyone you want, as long as *Morning Song* approves.

"We are not your bosses anymore," Ray said. "It is your ship, you have your mission, you do as you see fit on that mission. But you do need to ask your ship."

Roscoe nodded. That made sense. *Morning Song* needed to be able to work with them.

"Without sitting in the chairs," Maria asked, "is there any way *Morning Song* can give them the knowledge about herself she gave us at first?"

"Any panel will tell them," Tacita said.

"But I would do that in private," Ray said, "since they will have a lot of questions."

"Do you think Fisher and Callie will agree?" Tacita asked Roscoe.

Roscoe smiled at Ray and Tacita. "You put the four of us together for a reason, didn't you?"

"We did," Ray said, smiling. "If Fisher and Callie agree, can we ask one thing?"

"Certainly," Maria said.

Roscoe knew exactly what Ray was going to ask, so he said it first. "You want them in forty years to chair the next Mother Ship coming in."

Again, Ray laughed. "Yes. But I would suggest you not tell them that, not at first at least."

Tacita nodded. "Wait five or ten thousand years."

Again Roscoe just couldn't imagine living that long. But he agreed anyway.

Two days later *Morning Song* had agreed to their choice of Fisher and Callie, and Fisher and Callie had agreed and said they were honored beyond words.

Then they had gone through the scanner brain widening in the Command Center and been stunned.

"I can actually see and understand the ship now," Fisher said, looking off into the distance in his mind.

Roscoe laughed at that, since that was exactly how he had felt.

"*Morning Song*," Callie said, "You are a masterpiece in construction and engineering."

The words *Thank You, Callie*, appeared on the big screen in the Command Center.

Maria hugged Callie at that.

That evening, in the kitchen of *The Lady*, while Fisher cooked a wonderful dinner in celebration, the four of them laughed and joked and then started to plan what was needed to be done over the next few years to get ready for the mission.

Ten days later, *Morning Song* had slowed enough to start bringing in more help.

The Huntington, with about half her crew staying, left to go start recruiting and setting up construction areas for the building of the warships needed.

Roscoe and Maria had put Red and Mattie in charge of the military wing of the mission and all the recruitment, since *Morning Song* had liked both of them and they both had agreed to go along when asked.

The plan that Roscoe and Maria and Fisher and Callie had worked out was pretty set. It would take almost five years to hire crew, do needed repairs, stock everything, and build enough ships to have a fighter fleet on board.

For Seeders, five years was a blink of an eye.

Chairman Ray thought that far too fast, but said he would wait and see.

For Roscoe, it seemed like a very long time.

But as long as he and Maria were together, time really didn't seem to matter.

SECTION FOUR:

THE MISSION CHANGE

CHAPTER 36

A month later, more and more crew were coming on board and fanning out into different areas of *Morning Song*, doing repairs and bringing up stations. A promise of flowing water was still a ways away, something both Roscoe and Maria could hardly wait to have happen. Then they would be able to furnish and actually move into their Chairmen's suite.

They spent a lot of days, evenings, and often late into the nights in the command chairs, linked in with everything going on over the ship, working to prioritize what needed to be done first and helping the repair crews where they could.

Everything was going well, but over the last few days, there was something that had been bothering Roscoe as it became clear that their plan was soon going to be in full forward motion very soon.

Another couple of months, *Morning Song* will have slowed enough to actually trans-tunnel jump to a large Seeder base in a satellite galaxy on the way to Andromeda where all major repairs and crew recruitment would really start.

And those preparations included building a large military fleet.

So one night, after he and Maria had spent a wonderful hour in their suite making love, he brought what was worrying him to Maria.

She was naked, her wonderful red hair spread over the bed, her shoulder cradled into his side, her arm over him and her leg over his leg. They often slept just like that, feeling more comfortable touching as much as they could.

He couldn't even remember or imagine being alone as he had before meeting her. That just seemed like an alien time and memory.

"I'm bothered by something," he said.

"Nothing I did, I hope," she said, snuggling even closer against him.

"Oh, heavens, no," he said, laughing and hugging her. "I'm worried that we are planning for a mission with million-year-old scouting data."

She pushed herself up on her elbow and looked into his eyes with those wonderful, round, golden eyes of hers.

"You suggesting we send a scouting mission?"

"No, I think you and I need to do it," he said. "We need to see what we are taking over a million people on the *Morning Song* into."

Now she frowned. "How? The target galaxy is over thirty galaxies away from here. We can't be gone that long from the preparations here. That would take a decade to get there and back at top trans-tunnel speeds."

"I know," he said, smiling at her.

She shook her head and laughed. "You have a plan, don't you?"

"I do," he said, smiling at her, "but it will take being in the Command Center and the help of *Morning Song* to lay it all out."

She pushed away from him and stood, her wonderful naked body shining in the dim light of the bedroom in their suite.

"Where are you going?" he asked, enjoying the view of her toned body and smooth skin and the patterns of freckles.

"We're not sleeping until we work this through," she said, grabbing her slacks she had shoved off to one side of the bed. "You want to present this idea to Fisher and Callie as well at the same time? They are still in Command Center."

He stood, laughing. This was not what he expected, but he should have. "Might as well."

She pulled on the thin, silk blouse she had been wearing earlier without the exercise bra, then said simply, "*Morning Song*, please warn Chairman Fisher that we will be arriving."

Five minutes later, after one long kiss that Maria said was to hold her, they jumped to Command Center.

CHAPTER 37

The moment Roscoe said that he was bothered by planning a mission on ancient scouting data, she knew he was right. And he seemed to have a way to scout the distant target galaxy without spending the years to get there.

Somehow. He was smart that way and could see patterns and solutions no one around him could see. One of the thousands of things she loved about him.

The overall mission was that *Morning Song* would seed galaxies along the way, getting close to the target galaxy in about one and a half million years. Maria was still having a very difficult time grasping those sorts of time spans, but yet it seemed very ambitious that they could completely seed an entire galaxy with human life in only fifty thousand years. But that was a normal time for Seeders.

In the Command Center, both Callie and Fisher stood as Maria and Roscoe appeared. They had both been working at their stations on either side of the big chairs. Both wore jeans and Fisher had on a dress shirt with his sleeves rolled up while Callie wore a white blouse with a necklace of freshwater pearls.

The Command Center felt like her home every time she came here. Even though it was a huge space, it felt intimate to Maria.

There were four other crew members in the room, so Roscoe turned to them and said, "Please take a break, everyone. Chairman Fisher will contact you when you can return."

All of them nodded and vanished.

"So what's happening?" Fisher asked, looking puzzled.

Maria smiled and sat on the empty chair for one of the environmental stations. "Roscoe has a plan he wants to run past the four of us and *Morning Song*.

"To do what?" Callie asked.

"We need to scout where we are headed," Roscoe said. "Before we make preparations we either don't need, or that are not enough."

Callie and Fisher both nodded.

Maria turned to face the big screen. "*Morning Song*, please bring up a two dimensional representation of the galaxies between the Milky Way and our target galaxy that are on the plan to seed."

On the screen the Milky Way was labeled. Then like stones crossing a river, the other galaxies and satellite galaxies along the way were marked, with a line from one to the other. The line stopped short of a galaxy marked with an X.

Maria had seen that image a number of times and studied it. If she really was as long-lived as it seemed she would be, barring accidents, that simple map represented the next million and a half years of her life.

Impossible for her to grasp, so she had made herself stop thinking about it.

"*Morning Song*, at a Seeder ship's fastest trans-tunnel pace," Roscoe said, "how long would it take to get to the target galaxy?"

The answer appeared on the screen below the map as a direct line appeared from the Milky Way to the target galaxy.

Seventy-one years.

"To your knowledge," Roscoe asked, "are there any Seeder ships between here and the target galaxy. If there are, explain what they are and show their locations."

. . .

Twelve scout ships.

Green dots appeared showing the locations of all the scout ships searching ahead for any sign of intelligent alien life.

Maria knew those ships were slightly smaller than Chairman Ray's ship and held a crew of a thousand or more. A couple of the scout ships were even larger and very fast. They were staffed with mostly scientists and explorers and their families, people who loved to push off into the unknown to see what they could find.

Those scout ships were very fast and only lightly armed, but had the best screens known to Seeder technology, so they could move around without ever being seen if there was alien life. She knew from the knowledge poured into her head that the scout ships often spent a couple hundred years or more in a galaxy.

The closest ship to the target galaxy was only two galaxies away from the target.

Suddenly Maria understood what Roscoe was thinking.

"*Morning Song,*" Maria asked. "At full speed, how long would it take the closest scout ship to reach the target galaxy?"

Approximately twenty-three days.

Roscoe was smiling.

Maria went over and kissed him, then hugged him. "That's just brilliant."

Fisher cleared his throat and then said, "We might need a little more explanation here."

Maria turned to the big screen again and pointed. "*Morning Song,* please connect each ship with each other ship, starting from the Milky Way."

Green lines connected the green dots.

"Is any distance between ships too far for Chairman Ray to transport?" Roscoe asked.

No.

You and Chairman Boone could also make the jumps.

Now that shocked Maria. She had no idea she had that ability. She wouldn't even begin to know how to do it. Just the idea of transporting herself over an entire galaxy gave her the shudders.

Beside her, Roscoe was staring at the big screen, shaking his head. Clearly he had not known he could do that either.

CHAPTER 38

R oscoe looked at Maria and smiled after he got over the shock of being told he could personally transport over distances between galaxies. He honestly didn't want to think about that at the moment.

Besides, he wanted Chairman Ray and Tacita to be part of this scouting mission as well.

But looking at the big screen, he suddenly realized something else that needed to be added to the upcoming mission, part of Maria's plan to help Seeders have more of a historical memory, even over millions of years.

"*Morning Song,*" Roscoe asked. "Approximately how far can a person who has been given training as a Seeder transport under normal conditions?"

Over one hundred thousand light years is standard

"Why that question?" Maria asked, looking puzzled.

"A new addition to our mission," Roscoe said. "We add in jump stations along our path so any of us can easily return to the Milky Way at any time."

She instantly understood what he was suggesting and again gave him a hug.

"That will help with the Seeder historical records," she said.

"And help us return to our lodge at times for rest periods," Fisher said, smiling. "Thank you."

Roscoe could tell that Fisher and Callie really, really liked that idea. Leaving their lodge was one of the only hesitations they had about joining the mission.

"It will also make recruiting for this mission much easier," Callie said.

"We'll call it *Project Breadcrumbs*," Maria said. "Each jump station can have shops, sleeping areas, restaurants, and so on."

He loved that and they all laughed, but he knew the name would stick. And he had to admit, it would help a lot with recruiting. Someone knowing they could return home at any moment was much better than trying to convince someone to never return.

"So when do we talk with Chairman Ray and Tacita," Maria asked, "about this scouting mission and jump station idea."

"How about now?" Roscoe asked. "If there are objections, I sure would like to hear them before we go any farther."

"So would I," Maria said.

She took Roscoe by the hand and pulled him down toward their chairs. He knew what she was doing. In the chairs, they could talk directly to Chairman Ray and ask him to come here if he was close. As far as Roscoe knew, Ray was close.

They sat down in the chair and a moment later were melded even more than they were outside the chair.

Roscoe loved that feeling.

He loved everything about being close to Maria.

"Chairman Ray?" Maria said aloud, knowing her voice was being sent to Ray. "Would you and Tacita have a few moments to talk with us in *Morning Song's* Command Center?"

"Certainly," Ray said, his image clear in the reply. "Five minutes."

He cut off and Roscoe stood, pulling Maria to her feet.

"Well?" Fisher asked.

"Chairman Ray is on the way," Roscoe said, turning to look up at the images still on the big screen. He had no doubt this coming conversation was going to be interesting. He just wasn't sure how or in which direction it would go.

"*Morning Song*, please clear your screen for the moment," Maria asked.

The big screen cleared.

Roscoe had no idea what he would do if Chairman Ray said no to this scouting idea. There was no way he was going to spend years preparing a mission without knowing a little of what they were facing.

He had been in the military far too long to do that. He wasn't going to take millions of humans on *Morning Song* into some huge disaster or fight without being prepared correctly.

And correctly meant he needed to know what they were going to face, even a million and a half years in the future.

CHAPTER 39

Maria was holding Roscoe's hand when Chairman Ray and Tacita appeared. Ray was in his standard gray slacks and silk dress shirt and Tacita had on dark pants and a white blouse that set off her black hair.

She looked stunning to Maria.

"Thank you for joining us," Roscoe said as Chairman Ray nodded to each of them.

They were all standing on the second deck behind the big chairs, Maria and Roscoe together, Ray and Tacita together, touching but not holding hands, and Callie and Fisher standing together.

"It is always a pleasure," Ray said. "So what can we help with?"

"We have two ideas that are linked," Roscoe said. "First, we hope to add into the overall mission the building of jump stations as we go along."

"Jump stations?" Tacita asked, frowning.

"Yes," Maria said, taking the lead with this idea, "stations on planets or in orbits or in deep space of some sort that we will design ahead that will allow any Seeder to jump back to the Milky Way and Local Group from any point along our mission. Or any galaxy we have left and recruited from as we move forward."

"Spaced about every one hundred thousand light years," Roscoe said, "a normal range that most Seeders can jump."

"It will help with my project of adding in a historical memory for Seeders," Maria said.

"And it will help in recruiting over the next few years," Fisher said.

"We call it *Project Breadcrumbs*," Maria said.

"Has that been tried before to your knowledge?" Roscoe asked.

Maria watched intently, her stomach twisting slightly as Chairman Ray glanced at Tacita, then shook his head.

"Such an obvious and good idea," Ray said, "but it has never been done to my knowledge."

"It is a very good idea," Tacita said. "Once the basic stations are designed, it could be fitted into the Local Group here as well, since all races in this area are still young and many Seeders would love to return at times to their home planets."

Roscoe smiled at Maria who squeezed his hand in excitement. She couldn't believe they liked the idea and that it had never been tried. Of course, Maria knew that if Roscoe hadn't thought of it, it still wouldn't be happening.

"I assume the second idea is the one that is in question," Chairman Ray said.

Roscoe nodded. "You recruited us because we were young and also had a military sense about our culture."

"That is correct," Ray said, nodding.

Maria was almost holding her breath she was so worried about this suddenly.

"So we need to act in a military fashion right now," Roscoe said.

Ray looked puzzled.

Tacita said flatly, "I do not understand what you mean."

"In any military situation," Roscoe said, "no army or soldier will ever go into a battle or mission without good advanced intelligence. Right now, we are planning this mission on extremely old data and that kind of reckless movement could well lead to disaster."

"What do you suggest?" Ray asked, his voice low and not cold, but not welcoming.

"We scout the target galaxy again, right now, so our preparations are in line with the threat we face," Roscoe said.

Maria turned to the big screen. "*Morning Song*, please put on the big screen the galaxies between here and the target galaxy."

The image of the Milky Way appeared with the galaxies between it and the target galaxy, again marked with a red "x" over it.

"Thank you, *Morning Song*," Maria said. "Now show the location of all Seeder Scout ships along that line."

The green dots appeared along the way.

"We can tell," Roscoe said, "at least from any reports coming from that lead scout ship, that the Lotus is not within two galaxies of that lead ship's position."

Ray nodded, looking up at the big screen. Then he frowned and shook his head.

Roscoe turned and looked directly at both Ray and Tacita. "I propose we jump to that lead scout ship and take a look at the Lotus galaxy before we go too much farther with large-scale plans to include a large military force on *Morning Song* when there is a good chance it won't be needed."

Maria could feel herself still holding her breath. This was one of those turning point moments and both she and Roscoe knew it. She wasn't sure how they had gone from making love to having a moment that might change decades and maybe centuries of work, but they had.

Ray stood there for a moment, then asked a simple question. "*Morning Song*, what is the name of that lead scout ship?"

On the big screen the words appeared over the images of the galaxy.

I do not know for certain, Chairman Ray

Maria watched as Ray nodded, then he said simply, "We will return in five minutes."

Tacita and Ray vanished, leaving the Command Center in silence.

Maria just shook her head and squeezed Roscoe's hand.

"When I'm that age," Fisher said, "I hope I explain my actions to the poor people around me a little better."

"When you're that age," Roscoe said, "you won't have to."

Maria laughed.

Fisher said, "Good point."

Then standing there in silence, Maria looked up at the screen and suddenly had a thought she didn't much like.

"*Morning Song*," Maria said. "How do you know the location of those ships? And do you know who sent them on those missions?"

The positions are their assigned projected positions at this point in time.

Chairman Ray sent them on the mission ahead of my being launched, ahead of the Seeder ships coming to the Local Group.

"Oh, crap," Fisher said softly.

Maria's stomach clamped up and she had a hunch their great idea to scout ahead had just been shot down.

"Are you telling me," Roscoe said, staring at the big board with disbelief, "that those scout ships have been out scouting for almost two million years?"

"Yes," Maria said softly.

"And that lead ship might not be there after all," Callie said, "or it might have been taken over by Lotus if they are expanding?"

"Yes," Chairman Ray said as he and Tacita appeared again. "That is exactly the result of using old data, as I have been asking you to do. That has been my problem and we need to correct that."

Maria stared at Ray for a moment, surprised at that statement.

"Do we even know if any of those ships are in those positions?" Roscoe asked.

"We do," Tacita said, "because being scout ships is their job and how they get paid. They scout and report back. Over the two millions years each of those ships has returned to a major Seeder galaxy many, many times for overhaul and updates of equipment. Scout ships always use the most advanced technology and have the best screens and speed."

"They also send a comprehensive report back every ten years," Ray said.

Ray turned to the big screen. "*Morning Song*, please contact my ship and update your records on this topic."

An instant later, on the screen about a third of the green dots vanished. But the ship two galaxies away from the target galaxy was still there.

"*The Horizon* is the name of that lead ship," Ray said. "It has over two thousand humans on board and is extremely fast and modern. Chairman Strong welcomes the use of his ship for such a scouting purpose you proposed, Chairman Mundy. He will have his ship under way at full speed toward the target galaxy in three hours. It will take just over twenty days for him to get there."

"How does he even know?" Maria asked, stunned, staring at the screen showing the incredible distance from the Milky Way over thirty galaxies to the solo green dot on the screen.

Ray just shrugged, as if that was a silly question. "I just spoke with him."

CHAPTER 40

Roscoe and Maria spent the next twenty days continuing almost day and night with the repairs to *Morning Song*.

And every day they found time to make love in their unfurnished suite. Maria insisted they spend that private time and Roscoe was not going to decline something like that with the most beautiful woman he had ever met.

And one he was head-over-feet in love with as well.

The crew on board had grown from the original fifteen to just over six hundred. And yet *Morning Song* still seemed completely empty to Roscoe.

Finally, after what seemed like an incredible task with more problems than Roscoe could ever imagine, the water systems on the ship had been completely repaired, recharged, flushed, and deemed safe. Having that system shut down and in near-zero temps had caused seemingly millions of problems. But now all the problems were fixed and it was functioning.

Finally, the original team could leave Fisher and Callie's wonderful ship, get their own places to live, and let Fisher and Callie have some peace.

So Roscoe and Maria spent a few hours in the morning in one of the huge warehouses, finding furniture for their suite.

And by that evening, it was furnished enough to live in. Even the fireplace was working. They had put very soft brown area rugs in certain places for contrast, and the kitchen was completely stocked. Maria had even found some incredible pictures of various worlds, framed in storage, and hung them on the walls.

She said as they visited new places together, they would replace them.

Roscoe had to admit, the place felt like home, a home he would enjoy for a very long time.

When Roscoe told Fisher that their kitchen was finally stocked and working, Fisher offered to cook the four of them the first meal in the new kitchen. Both Roscoe and Maria had taken him up on that instantly, since they had come to love his cooking and Fisher loved to cook.

Maria said it was better to start off their new kitchen with a quality meal instead of something either she or Roscoe could do.

And the meal had been wonderful. Great chicken dinner with great friends and lots of laughter. Nothing could have better for the first full meal in their new home.

Then next morning, Roscoe told Fisher and Callie to take good care of *Morning Song*, and he and Maria jumped to Chairman Ray's ship.

The Command Center there felt very small compared to *Morning Song's*. Roscoe was stunned he had been getting used to the huge size so quickly.

Ray and Tacita were standing there in front of the big screen. And both nodded to them as they appeared.

Roscoe had no idea what might happen. He knew that being so far away from known homes bothered him more than he wanted to admit. Sort of feeling like he was out in an ocean and couldn't see land.

Of course, over the next million plus years, all the galaxies they were going to jump over would be seeded with human life, by a ship and crews he controlled. But in the meantime, there just wasn't anything in any of them. All scout ships had come up completely empty for any intelligent alien life in any of the galaxies.

"We're only taking the four of us," Ray said. "And I'm going to jump us all the way to *The Horizon*. They are nearing the border of the target galaxy."

Maria glanced at Roscoe and took his hand. Clearly she was as worried about this as he was.

Roscoe just nodded and Ray reached over and took Tacita's hand in his. Then he smiled and a moment later the four of them were standing in a very modern Command Center.

There were seven crew in the room, four manning stations on the upper level, three at stations on the middle level. The place was pure white and what metal there was shined.

As they appeared, everyone stood and bowed slightly.

Then a young man with a beaming smile and short, blonde hair stepped forward from near the center command chair. "It is an honor to have you on board, Chairmen."

"The honor is ours," Chairman Ray said, bowing slightly.

Roscoe had no idea what all the bowing was about, but at some point he needed to ask someone.

Then Ray turned to Tacita. "Chairman Strong, you know Tacita?"

Strong bowed slightly again. "Always a pleasure."

Tacita bowed back.

Ray pointed to Roscoe and Maria where they stood holding hands. "Chairmen Mundy and Boone of *Morning Song*."

Strong's eyes got large and Roscoe was surprised at that kind of reaction. He bowed once again and said, "We are honored."

Roscoe didn't know what to say, so Maria jumped in. "We are the ones who are honored that you gave this mission such important attention."

"Yes, very much," Roscoe said.

With that, Strong nodded to one of his crew and turned around and pointed at the big screen. "Let me show you what we have found so far. We are within a few hours of the edge of the target galaxy at this speed and we are completely shielded."

On the screen a large mass of stars appeared. Roscoe knew the galaxy was a cluster galaxy that sat alone, with no secondary galaxies or satellite galaxies even close. It had about the same number of stars as the Milky Way, but there was no telling how many were suited for life. Cluster galaxies tended to have fewer on average than spiral galaxies.

"Long-range scans are showing no signs of any forms of extremely advanced cultures at all."

"Nothing?" Ray asked, sounding surprised.

"Nothing so far, sir," Strong said.

"That should not be the case," Ray said.

Roscoe wasn't surprised at all. But he didn't want to tell Ray that. Over the last few hundred years, and especially in the last forty working in the Sector Justice force, Roscoe had seen how short-lived dictators and totalitarian governments were. They often destroyed themselves quickly, even without Seeder help.

A huge ship full of humans had arrived here more millions of years ago than Roscoe wanted to think about. If they had managed to establish a stable, war-like culture, he would have been very, very surprised and worried. He was pretty sure a culture like that wasn't possible for more than a few hundred years.

But still, the chance of that was why they were here. And that fear was why Chairman Ray had sent the *Morning Song* and picked him and Maria.

But the chance was not great anything remained here.

"Any sign of where the *Dark Night* might be located?" Tacita asked.

"Yes," Strong said.

The image on the big screen focused in on a cluster of stars just inside the edge of the galaxy. "We located one of the beacons on it you said would be there, Chairman Ray. We will be in the same system thirty minutes after entering the galaxy."

Ray nodded and Roscoe felt stunned. Maria's hand gripped his tightly.

The big ship that had brought the Lotus here millions and millions of years ago was instantly found even from this distance. Amazing.

"How?" Maria asked.

"We planted numbers of signal systems in the big ship," Tacita said, "that would last and could not be traced."

"Is there a place we could wait and watch your scans and approach and not be in the way?" Ray asked.

Strong nodded. "Yes. I can jump you there if you don't mind."

Ray nodded and a moment later the five of them were in a large conference room with screens on all four walls and all sorts of stations around the walls.

Roscoe glanced around at the very comfortable space. In the center of the room was a white conference table with comfortable cloth chairs around it and doughnuts and other baked goods, along with fruit, on the table. There were also pitchers of water and glasses.

All the screens came up live at that moment and Strong pointed to one in the center. "You'll be able to follow us in Command Center there and all major scans and data will appear on the other screens.

"This is wonderful," Tacita said, looking around.

"Yes, thank you, Chairman," Ray said.

"My pleasure and my ship's honor," he said. "Now if you will excuse me."

At that he jumped away and appeared in the Command Center, quickly sitting down in his command chair.

Roscoe could tell that Chairman Strong was as excited as he was feeling, maybe more, since he and his ship existed to explore new places. And this galaxy was about as new and different as it got.

CHAPTER 41

After an hour or more, Maria had given in and taken a doughnut and some water. The stress of watching and waiting was more than she could take. She wasn't sure if the chocolate-covered cake doughnut would help, but they had smelled so good, she had to find out.

More than anything else she wanted to get up and pace, but she forced herself to sit and eat instead. And luckily, the doughnut tasted as good as it smelled and was very fresh. And the dark chocolate was her favorite.

Roscoe sat in the chair next to her, staring at mostly only three screens, all showing visuals ahead. She could tell he was in his military mindset and not moving at all.

Ray and Tacita sat near the end of the table, one chair separating the two couples. They were also staring at the screens, swiveling around at times to take in other readings from other scans.

Maria was about halfway through the doughnut when Chairman Ray turned to them. "What did you expect to find here?"

Maria had had no expectations, but she knew what Roscoe had expected, so she nodded to him.

"Not much," Roscoe said. "But we had to know for sure, otherwise we would have prepared *Morning Song* completely wrong for her coming mission to seed."

"Why did you not expect any problems here?" Tacita asked.

"For the same reason you picked me and Maria for this task," Roscoe said. "I know military and dictatorships, and I know that is not a cultural structure that can sustain even over short periods of time, as you proved in the original galaxy. You won and sent the survivors here."

"Freedom of choice and a desire to make a profit will always win in the end," Maria said, then licked chocolate from her fingers.

"So what exactly are you expecting?" Ray asked after glancing at the screens once again.

"Ravaged and destroyed planets, maybe, that might be so destroyed as to not be overgrown with local plants. There might be small enclaves of humans, if any. Very low technology, if any."

Maria watched Ray nodding to that.

Roscoe went on. "Considering the millions of years they have been here, and logically spread out some at first, we might find a stable culture growing similar to what we plant."

"Seriously?" Tacita asked.

Roscoe nodded. "From survivors. But if they continued to develop without help, my gut sense is that they will just keep falling into the same patterns we all know so well that cultures go through."

"And thus end up destroying each other," Maria said, trying to decide to go for another doughnut or not.

Ray frowned.

"Seeding the planets is wonderful," Maria said, finally leaning forward to take another fantastic chocolate doughnut, "but it would be for nothing if not for the Seeders who remain behind for hundreds of thousands of years and guide the cultures up through the turmoil and the instability. That makes all the difference."

"Entering the edge of the galaxy now," Chairman Strong said over a ship-wide broadcast system. "Stay alert, everyone. Thirty minutes to first target."

Now that got Maria's full attention.

And made her even more nervous.

She bit into the wonderful chocolate cake doughnut, then grabbed a couple of napkins. Chewing, she put the doughnut down on a napkin and turned her full attention to the screens. Especially the one indicating the signal coming from the *Dark Night*, the huge prison ship that had brought millions to this distant galaxy.

CHAPTER 42

oscoe studied the screens as *The Horizon* dropped out of trans-tunnel flight. On the screen beside the image of the Command Center, the dark image of the old ship appeared. Small at first, and then the image got closer and closer and larger.

He didn't know what to expect, but was surprised the ship looked almost round, with engines on one flattened side, not at all normal Seeder shapes.

But, of course, this was long before the idea of seeding outside the original galaxy had come about and the bird design of Seeder ships.

As the image got in closer, there was little doubt that the ancient ship was barely holding together. Giant meteors had smashed into it from all sides over the years. The only reason it still existed was because it was away from any orbit of any planet or large moon and no gravitational forces were pulling on it.

"Stunning any beacon still worked," Roscoe said, more to himself.

"Only one survived out of a hundred," Ray said. "We built them into bulkheads and in the metal walls of the ship itself."

"Wow," Maria said.

On another screen, it was clear that what had been an Earth-like planet close to the big ship was nothing but a burnt and destroyed husk.

Roscoe had no doubt something very ugly had happened on that planet, more than likely human-caused a very long time ago. No atmosphere remained at all.

"Chairman Ray, would you and the other Chairmen please come to the Command Center."

Roscoe glanced around at the other screens quickly before Ray jumped them to the Command Center.

"We are getting some very interesting scans from different areas of this galaxy," Chairman Strong said, not getting up from his chair.

The big screen focused on a star about sixty light-years away from where they had found the big ship. "A planet around this sun has a flourishing human society on it, early space age levels."

"Can we take a closer look?" Ray asked.

"There's something else," Strong said, "that you need to know before we move. We are showing preliminary scans of two different alien races in this galaxy as well. Both about the same technological level as the human society."

The image on the screen pulled back and Roscoe could see that one race was on the far side of the galaxy, the other only about four hundred light years from the young human society.

"We have no idea what kind of cultures they are from this distance," Strong said.

Ray was looking as shocked as Roscoe felt.

Ray looked at his wife for a moment, then turned to Strong. "We need to clear historical evidence that humans came to this galaxy from the outside. Can we bump the remains of *Dark Night* into a path that will take it into the sun?"

"We can," Strong said. "It will take a couple weeks to get it moving without tearing it apart."

"Can you consider that part of your mission now, Chairman?" Ray asked Strong. "And destroying any other historical evidence of the Lotus coming from outside this galaxy."

Strong nodded. "That is no problem."

"Can we take a look at the advanced civilizations safely?" Roscoe asked.

"Please," Ray asked Strong, who nodded and then indicated that his crew jump to trans-tunnel flight.

Within minutes they were back in real space, approaching the human population.

"Early space age," Strong said, nodding.

Roscoe noted that Strong glanced around at one of his crew on the bridge. The brown-haired woman shook her head and looked back at her board.

"Without help," Strong said, staring at his screen at his command chair, "they will destroy themselves and this planet in the next decade. If not sooner. They are in the standard human society growth pattern almost perfectly."

"Then we need to get some help here quickly," Maria said.

"Why would we do that?" Tacita said, frowning and looking at Maria. "They are Lotus."

Roscoe actually laughed. "Millions and millions of years ago their ancestors were Lotus. But now they are just a new human planet trying to get started and they need help to survive and follow a path to stability."

"We're Seeders, aren't we?" Maria asked, staring at Tacita. "Helping young human cultures get started on the right road is part of our job description."

Tacita started to open her mouth, then closed it. Roscoe could tell that Maria's words had hit home and got through the millions of years of thinking anyone in this galaxy would still hold the beliefs from so long before.

Chairman Ray had a slight grin on his face, but said nothing.

Strong looked between the four of them, then said, "Many of my people were trained in planetary cultural growth. We're going to be in this galaxy giving it a good scouring for a good two hundred years, if not more. We can help them until better help arrives."

"Thank you, Chairman Strong," Ray said, bowing. "You and your crew will be justly rewarded, I can promise."

"Thank you, Chairman," Strong said.

"Please send regular reports every month for the next few years,"

Ray said. "I'm going to be following this very interesting galaxy's progress with great attention."

"As am I," Roscoe said.

Strong nodded.

"And I really am curious as to the other alien races," Ray said. "A very unusual find. Thank you for your ship's work on this. And your time. It is very much appreciated."

A moment later the four of them were back in the Command Center of Ray's ship, over thirty galaxies away.

Roscoe still couldn't wrap his mind around how that was done. He was just glad Ray was good at it.

Chairman Ray turned to Roscoe and Maria. "It seems we have a mission statement to change."

"Thankfully, yes," Roscoe said. "And I have some ideas."

"As do I," Maria said, smiling.

Tacita actually smiled at that.

Chairman Ray stared at both of them for a moment. "Nothing can substitute for the excitement of youth. I will be looking forward to the new ideas."

Roscoe took Maria's hand. Then with a nod, he jumped them back to the *Morning Song* Command Center, much to the surprise of Fisher and Callie, who expected them to be gone much, much longer.

SECTION FIVE:

THE FUTURE

CHAPTER 43

Maria just couldn't get enough of Roscoe, and forced them to spend private time together every day, even though they had a million things to get done and worked together all day.

She felt they needed the time.

And they both enjoyed it. She was stunned, but she kept feeling closer and closer and more in love with Roscoe every day. She didn't think this kind of depth of love was even possible.

Since the scouting missing, she and Roscoe and Callie and Fisher had spent many meals planning what exactly to do with all the extra space that Ray had designed into *Morning Song* for a huge fleet of military craft.

Part of the space, Maria was happy to see, would be converted into making jump stations for the *Breadcrumbs* project. But that took up such a small part of the huge space that Ray had planned for a military fleet, it didn't seem to really dent the empty areas.

Ten days after they returned, while having dinner in their suite—a wonderful dinner Fisher cooked of stream trout, garlic potatoes, and steamed vegetables—she and Roscoe decided to tell Fisher and Callie about the *Morning Breeze*, the second big empty Mother Ship coming into the galaxy in forty years.

"Ray and Tacita hope you two will be the Chairmen of *Morning Breeze*."

Fisher just blinked.

Callie said simply, "What?"

Both were stunned.

Maria loved it, since Fisher and Callie knew what being joint Chairmen of a Seeder Mother Ship meant.

They had just finished eating and were talking about the next day's major tasks as they cleaned up when suddenly Maria had an idea.

"You guys want to indulge me for a moment in the Command Center?"

Roscoe looked at her and raised his eyebrows.

She punched his arm. "Not that kind of indulge. I got an idea that will take help from *Morning Song* to figure out if it is even possible."

"Last time we did this, we ended up thirty galaxies away from here," Roscoe said, smiling.

"I don't think this is that far," Maria said, smiling at the three laughing friends.

They jumped into Command Center, much to the surprise of the crew working the evening shift.

"Would everyone please take a break until we call you back?" Callie asked.

The five who had been on duty nodded and vanished.

"*Morning Song*," Callie said, turning to the big screen that at the moment was totally blank. "In your updates from Chairman Ray's ship, have you pinpointed the location of *Morning Breeze*. If so, would you show us?"

On the big screen the image of the Local Group of galaxies appeared, clearly showing the Milky Way and their position.

A dotted line extended backwards and ended with a green light labeled *Morning Breeze*. It seemed to be numbers of galaxies away. And at mostly sub-light speeds and only short trans-tunnel jumps as *Morning Song* had been doing, Maria could see how that distance would take forty thousand years.

"At the top speed of *The Lady*," Maria asked, "how long would it take to reach the *Morning Breeze* in trans-tunnel flight?"

The stunning words appeared on the screen.

Thirty-one days.

Maria turned and looked at the shocked expression on the other three faces. Then she said simply, "Now we have some real planning to do."

CHAPTER 44

O ver the next week, while still slowing *Morning Song* and getting more and more help on board to work on the major repairs and getting areas of the ship staffed, the four of them met every evening over dinner to plan.

Roscoe enjoyed those dinners more than he wanted to admit.

And they often ended up in the Command Center of *Morning Song* using the big screen to get some scale of the different galaxies where their seeding mission was heading.

On the seventh night of dinner meetings, Roscoe was thinking about the paths of future seeding missions when a different image appeared in his mind.

A balloon.

And he said that out loud.

At the moment he had been handing dishes to Maria to put into the dishwasher in their suite and Fisher and Carrie were still sitting at the now cleared table.

Maria looked at him with a puzzled frown? "Balloon?"

He nodded and handed her the last plate he had rinsed, then dried off his hands and moved over to his spot at the table.

"You know how we are always saying that Seeders think big."

Fisher made an arm gesture. "I think *Morning Song* is an example of that."

"And the fact that they have been doing this for more millions of years than I care to think about," Maria said.

"What happens if they aren't thinking big enough?" Roscoe asked.

"Now you are starting to scare me a little," Callie said.

Maria looked completely puzzled.

"Time to head for the Command Center," Roscoe said, smiling. "There is something that Tacita said at one point that has haunted me and I think I might have an answer."

A few minutes later they were there and the regular crew had taken a break.

Roscoe pointed to the big screen. "*Morning Song,*" he said, "please put the Milky Way at the center of a sphere and slowly expand out the sphere until the edge of the sphere hits the closest galaxy outside the Local Group."

On the big screen that image appeared, with a dotted line circle. It hit a galaxy that they all knew had been seeded already.

"Thank you, *Morning Song.*" Roscoe said. "Now please expand that sphere exactly one hundred thousand light years in radius."

"The distance of a jump station," Maria said and Roscoe smiled at her and nodded.

"Are there any unseeded galaxies in that sphere?"

"No," appeared on the screen.

"Please keep expanding the sphere by one hundred thousand light years in radius and put the number of unseeded galaxies at the bottom with every expansion. Stop at five expansions."

At two hundred thousand light-years, the numbers of unseeded galaxies was finally three.

At three hundred, it jumped to eight.

At four hundred it jumped to fourteen.

At five hundred thousand light years in radius from the center of the Milky Way, the number of unseeded galaxies jumped to eighteen.

"What exactly are you saying?" Fisher asked Roscoe.

Maria studied the image on the big screen for a second and then turned to Roscoe as well.

"We have been snaking our way outward as Seeders," Roscoe said. "Always just jumping to the closest galaxy ahead without a lot of thought. With the *Breadcrumbs* transport stations, why do that? Why not make the Milky Way the center of this expansion and move outward in a consistent sphere pattern."

He looked around at his friends and at the woman he loved. All three of them were blinking.

He went on. "The second deck can be a complete construction deck for building more Seeder ships as we go. We can have an entire factory working on both *Morning Song* and *Morning Breeze*. With the hundreds of frontline Seeder ships now working Andromeda, the frontline Seeder ships we have here, and the other Seeder frontline ships on *Morning Breeze*, we can do this easily if we keep building."

"And with the transport system, the entire bubble of Seeded galaxies can be held together," Maria said.

"Exactly," Roscoe said. "Tacita said that they needed so many more Seeder Mother Ships. Why not have a base here building more Seeder Mother Ships as the bubble expands and we need more?"

"And each Seeder Mother Ship would have a factory on it as well," Fisher said, nodding.

Maria moved closer and kissed him, sending shivers through him. Then she held him at arm's length and looked at him with those huge golden eyes. "That mind of yours continues to amaze me."

"Scares hell out of me," Fisher said.

CHAPTER 45

Maria lay naked, tucked under Roscoe's arm two hours later. The lights of their wonderful suite were dimmed and they had made love and then settled down to get some sleep. She felt relaxed and satisfied and completely at ease with her life and her world.

She loved just being against Roscoe, touching his skin, listening to him breathe, enjoying his faint musky smell. She could never seem to get enough of him, and when they were in the big command chairs and linked through *Morning Song,* it felt even better.

She opened one eye and looked at him. He seemed to be sleeping and she needed to sleep as well. But she just couldn't turn her mind off yet.

She was trying to remember not knowing Roscoe Mundy, her life before the last two months. And even though that had been hundreds of years of living, those times seemed like distant memories now compared to the last two months.

How was that possible?

And if the idea of expanding out in a sphere was accepted, with the transport stations, they were going to start an intergalactic culture that would stay in touch, learn from each planet, each culture, each galaxy, and continue to advance into levels she couldn't begin to imagine.

Just the idea of that had her excited beyond words.

And she and Roscoe and *Morning Song* would be on the leading edge of the building.

"Are you all right?" Roscoe asked her, hugging her closer.

She snuggled down even more against his smooth skin and hard muscles of his chest. "I'm about as all right as I can be," she said, softly.

"So what were you thinking about?"

"Honestly," she said, "about what we are going to build and about how much I love you."

"I really like both of those thoughts," he said, hugging her even tighter against him. "You know, we've never really talked about that we are committing ourselves to each other for a very long time."

"Does that bother you?" she asked.

He laughed softly. "It actually is one of the things I love about doing all this. I'm going to get to do this for a very, very long time with you."

She kissed him on the chest and said, "I like that thought as well."

"How about you?" he asked. "Are you bothered by us being together for such a long time?"

"I'm worried about one thing," she said, snuggling down against him.

"And what's that?" he asked.

"I'm worried that a very, very long time won't be long enough."

"Then we'll make it even longer," he said, squeezing her. "I promise."

"I promise as well," she said.

And with that she kissed his skin one more time and snuggled down close and went to sleep with the man she loved and planned to love for even more than an eternity.

USA TODAY BESTSELLING AUTHOR

DEAN WESLEY
SMITH

THE HIGH EDGE

A SEEDERS UNIVERSE NOVEL

If you enjoyed *Morning Song*, try the next thrilling novel in the Seeders
Universe series, *The High Edge*! What follows is a sample chapter.

CHAPTER 1

Somehow Benny Slade survived almost everyone else in the world dying.

One minute he went into his old steel vault that filled the back room at Benny's Personal Loans to get some cash for his next loan and when he came out, both Madge and Maggie, his two right hands, were laying face down on his newly installed brown carpet in the front office.

Madge, who looked more like his old mother used to look before she got hit by that cab, had fallen next to her always-neat and clean desk while Maggie, about two years younger than Benny's twenty-eight years, had sprawled in the middle of the floor, her short skirt riding up and showing him a little of those wonderful white panties of hers that he liked so much.

He had just come out of the vault with the two hundred and sixty in cash for Mrs. Tenny's loan. He dropped the money on his desk and just acted, not thinking.

First he called out to Maggie and kneeled beside her and checked her first. He couldn't find a pulse and she wasn't breathing.

Then he jumped over beside Madge. Same thing.

No pulse, no breathing.

Both were dead.

He sat back on his heels, still beside Madge.

He could feel that cold, hard feeling coming over him like it did when he had been in a firefight in Iraq.

He hadn't felt that in four long years.

He had hoped he would never feel it again.

With that cold, hard feeling, emotions got shoved back. He had needed that to happen in the gulf and it happened now.

He just stared at the two bodies in front of him.

What had happened? No one had come in or out because the bell hadn't rung on the door. And he had only been in the vault for less than thirty seconds.

It took him a good twenty seconds of staring at his two dead friends to figure out what was different, what was wrong besides two healthy women being suddenly dead.

He just kept kneeling there, staring until he finally saw it.

There was no blood.

Nothing.

They just lay face up, eyes wide open, completely dead.

"Move, Benny," he said out loud. That finally got himself into motion.

He stood and went to the phone and called 911, staring at the two women on the floor while he waited.

But no one answered.

With the phone to his ear, he went back and checked both of them again.

Very dead.

Very.

The phone was still ringing at the emergency center.

What had happened?

His first thought was gas attack, which got him moving even faster.

He took the phone and scrambled back into the vault.

He had left the vault door slightly open when he came out, so if it was some sort of terrorist gas attack, he was as good as dead as well.

Besides, he had stayed out in that front office for a good minute staring at his two friends and trying to call for help.

After fifteen seconds of standing in the dark working slowly to control his breathing, he got disgusted at himself.

"Come on, Benny, get it together. Do a little thinking. Use your damn head."

Madge had always complained he talked to himself too much, but Maggie thought it cute.

Maggie had thought anything he did cute, and he had thought she was cute.

They had flirted since the first day he hired her six months before. She was as sharp as they came and knew money and books and computers, even though she hadn't finished more than a year of high school. He was attracted but had managed to keep the relationship on only flirt level.

She had been fun, just not his type.

Even though he came across as the military type, he had two degrees from the City University of New York, including one in math. He liked women to be much, much smarter than Maggie. But she had still been fun to flirt with.

He went back out and stared at the two women on the floor. The phone to the emergency center was still ringing.

He hung it up and tried again.

It just kept ringing.

911 was slow at times in New York, but not that slow.

He didn't hang it up, just sat it on the desk and stared at Maggie there on the carpet for a moment. He was going to miss those white panties she flashed at him all day.

He was also going to miss her laugh and her smile and that wonderful blonde hair.

The coldness inside him whelmed upwards and he pushed those thoughts away. As his sergeant used to say, "Time to fight, time to think later if you survive the fight."

His sergeants over the years, all of them, had always been annoyed that he thought too much and didn't react quick enough when needed.

Clearly, this was some sort of strange fight he was in. He needed to get moving.

He turned away from Maggie and headed for the door.

At first, he opened the door slowly, not sure what to expect.

The moment the door cracked open, the wave of sound hit him like a hammer. He hadn't noticed that before because he always just blocked out any sounds from a New York street. Anyone living in the city needed that ability or otherwise go stark raving crazy.

He opened the door completely and stepped outside, going down the four small steps to the sidewalk.

The day was comfortable for an early summer day, with high overcast clouds that threatened rain. It wasn't very warm at all and wasn't supposed to turn hot for over a week. He hadn't been looking forward to the heat because he normally wore jeans, a long-sleeved shirt, and a sports coat over his shirt. Today he had on a tan shirt and dark-brown sports jacket.

But when the city turned into a giant sweat-box, he couldn't dress the way he liked and that just irked him.

He stood and took a deep breath of the cool afternoon air. Then he made himself really look at what was around him.

Up and down the street and on all the side streets hundreds and hundreds of car alarms and sirens were all going off at the same time.

Drivers were still in their cars, either slumped over, or head rolled to one side, held up by their seat belts. Cars had piled into intersections, had smashed into parked cars, or run up and against buildings.

Most car engines were still running, some racing as if their occupant still had a foot on the gas. Up Lexington Avenue he could see a fire starting to take hold of a building.

But what he didn't hear through all the noise were police and ambulance sirens.

And no one around him in the cars or on the sidewalk was moving.

No one.

This was some bad shit. Of that he had no doubt.

He quickly checked a couple of young girls on the sidewalk near his office front door to be sure they were dead. One had on a short blue skirt that had ridden up when she fell to show no underwear and he covered her up before checking her.

They were as gone as Madge and Maggie, eyes open.

He stared at their faces. They had not died in pain, that much he could tell.

No wonder no one had answered his call at the emergency number. From the looks of this, they were dead as well.

Then, up the street, he saw some movement as people came up out of the subway and sort of stopped and stared.

"So I'm not the only one," he said, feeling fantastically relieved.

He started toward the other people, then saw a couple of them panic and flee back down into the subway, followed by the others.

"Won't help," he shouted. But no one was going to hear anything over the noise of the car alarms and engines.

But they were doing exactly as he had done when he ran back into his old vault.

He glanced around at the buildings towering over the canyon of Lexington Ave. He couldn't see one window opening, or anyone even peaking out at all the noise.

And as far as he could see in both directions, everything was stopped and bodies covered the sidewalks.

He walked up to the corner of 54th, carefully walking around the bodies. He looked both directions.

Same thing along the tree-lined street.

Everyone was dead, knocked down by some sort of giant killer in an instant.

From what he could tell, not a one knew what hit them. None of them looked shocked or panicked or were showing any fear at all.

Just normal expressions on very dead people.

"What happened?" he asked out loud, but the words barely made it to his own ears in the noise of alarms and running cars.

Who knew that the end of the world was going to be so damned loud.

"I need to find out how far this spreads," he said into the noise.

He could feel the panic he had learned to hold down when he was a kid in fights on the street and when in the Iraq war start to ease up into his gut. He hadn't felt that in many years. It wasn't the dead bodies that bothered him.

He had seen worse.

Much worse.

Dead bodies after the first few months in Iraq had stopped bothering him, at least on the surface. His counselor at the VA said he had a lot of buried anger and that the only way to get healthy was to let out some of the anger and tell the counselor what he had seen.

He didn't want to tell anyone, so he and counselor hadn't gotten too far in the last few years.

Death didn't really scare Benny, but there were dead bodies on his street, in his own business, and he was still alive.

Now that scared hell out of him.

He started to head back to lock up his vault, then laughed and looked around. Unless this was the second coming and everyone was going to suddenly spring back to life, locking up his money was the least of his worries.

But he went in and locked the vault anyway, tossing the money back inside that he had taken out to loan Mrs. Tenny for her grandkid's operation. More than likely Mrs. Tenny and her grandkid weren't going to be needing much of anything anymore.

NEWSLETTER SIGN-UP

Follow Dean on BookBub

Be the first to know!

Just sign up for the Dean Wesley Smith newsletter, and keep up with the latest news, releases and so much more—even the occasional giveaway.

So, what are you waiting for? To sign up go to deanwesleysmith.com.

But wait! There's more. Sign up for the WMG Publishing newsletter, too, and get the latest news and releases from all of the WMG authors and lines, including Kristine Kathryn Rusch, Kristine Grayson, Kris Nelscott, *Pulphouse Fiction Magazine, Smith's Monthly,* and so much more.

To sign up go to wmgpublishing.com.

ABOUT THE AUTHOR

Considered one of the most prolific writers working in modern fiction, *USA Today* bestselling writer Dean Wesley Smith published far more than a hundred novels in forty years, and hundreds of short stories across many genres.

At the moment he produces novels in several major series, including the time travel Thunder Mountain novels set in the Old West, the galaxy-spanning Seeders Universe series, the urban fantasy Ghost of a Chance series, a superhero series starring Poker Boy, and a mystery series featuring the retired detectives of the Cold Poker Gang.

His monthly magazine, *Smith's Monthly*, which consists of only his own fiction, premiered in October 2013 and offers readers more than 70,000 words per issue, including a new and original novel every month.

During his career, Dean also wrote a couple dozen *Star Trek* novels, the only two original *Men in Black* novels, Spider-Man and X-Men novels, plus novels set in gaming and television worlds. Writing with his wife Kristine Kathryn Rusch under the name Kathryn Wesley, he wrote the novel for the NBC miniseries The Tenth Kingdom and other books for *Hallmark Hall of Fam*e movies.

He wrote novels under dozens of pen names in the worlds of comic books and movies, including novelizations of almost a dozen films, from *The Final Fantasy* to *Steel* to *Rundown*.

Dean also worked as a fiction editor off and on, starting at Pulphouse Publishing, then at *VB Tech Journal*, then Pocket Books, and now at WMG Publishing, where he and Kristine Kathryn Rusch serve as series editors for the acclaimed *Fiction River* anthology series.

For more information about Dean's books and ongoing projects, please visit his website at www.deanwesleysmith.com and sign up for his newsletter.

For more information:
www.deanwesleysmith.com

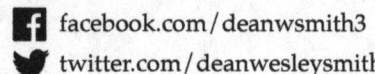 facebook.com/deanwsmith3
twitter.com/deanwesleysmith

www.ingramcontent.com/pod-product-compliance
Lightning Source LLC
Chambersburg PA
CBHW010734100726
47899CB00009B/3048